BELLE

takes

FLIGHT

Disney

BELLE *takes* FLIGHT

by Kathy McCullough
Random House 🏠 New York

For young book lovers everywhere

CHAPTER 1

$\mathbb{B}$elle ran her finger across the colorful spines of the books on a bottom shelf in the royal library, hoping to find one she'd missed. But no, they were the same books as when she'd last checked.

The library in the Prince's castle was so grand it seemed possible it could contain a copy of every book ever written. Yet there were only a few books on its towering shelves for the children who came

to Belle's weekly story time, and Belle had already read them aloud several times.

She'd also shared with them her favorite childhood book, *The Kingdom in the Clouds* by Pierre LeFaux, which she had brought with her when she and her father moved into the castle. The book was about a girl named Marie who traveled by dragon to a palace in the sky. Belle had now read it to the village children often enough that they knew it nearly as well as she did.

Belle brushed a strand of brown hair out of her eyes and gazed around the giant library. It seemed ridiculous to say, considering the hundreds of volumes in view, but she needed more books. That was why she'd asked the Prince to fund the construction of a library in the village. She planned to stock it with dozens of new children's books. But although the library was nearly complete, no books had yet arrived. There were only a few printing presses in France, and when you lived in a

small village like Villeneuve, you had to wait.

Belle wished there was something more she could do to get books for the village children. She slid the library ladder to another set of shelves. Maybe there was a children's book she'd missed, misfiled among the books on science and the biographies of adventurers.

She'd just begun to climb the ladder when—

BOOM!

The walls of the library shook from a blast. Belle gripped the ladder to keep herself from being thrown off.

A moment later, Cogsworth, the head of the castle's staff, burst into the room. "Your father—he is—I can't—" Cogsworth stammered, his pencil mustache twitching furiously. "He has to stop. This can*not*—"

"I'm sorry," Belle said as she climbed down. "I warned you when Papa moved his work-shop here—"

"I have a castle to run, mademoiselle!" Cogsworth tugged on his vest self-importantly—or rather, he *tried* to. The vest hugged his considerable belly so tightly he could barely get a grip on it. "But I can't run it if it's blown up!"

"I'm sure it was just a *little* explosion," Belle assured him—though when it came to her father, Maurice, she knew there was no such thing as a "little" explosion.

Belle urged Cogsworth to return to his work and promised she'd talk to her father. She dashed up the marble staircase, then hurried through the cavernous halls of the East Wing to the Prince's former nursery, which had been transformed into Maurice's workshop. Near the back wall, Maurice and the Prince were examining a huge metal contraption, too caught up in their task to notice their visitor.

Both men appeared unharmed—although the same couldn't be said of the room, which was

littered with springs, sprockets, nuts, and bolts. The doors of the cupboards lining the walls had been flung open, and the Prince's childhood toys and games were thrown everywhere.

Chip, the four-year-old son of Mrs. Potts, the castle cook, appeared in the doorway behind Belle. He gaped at the mess, but Belle just shook her head. "What went wrong *this* time?" she asked.

Maurice looked up from his invention and smiled. "Belle!"

As he ran to greet her, Belle noticed that his clothes were dripping with dirty water. "Papa! You're soaked!"

"A little problem with the steam-release valve," Maurice explained. "The water in the pipes got too hot, and . . . well, you know what happens when you get 'boiling mad' and can't 'blow off steam'?"

"You explode?" Belle asked with a wry smile.

Maurice tapped his nose to indicate that Belle had guessed correctly. "The side of the boiler blew

right off! Then one of the pipes hit the tool rack. The rack fell onto the cabinet with all my spare parts—and the next thing I knew, there were brackets and clamps everywhere!"

"That's power!" exclaimed the Prince, who was also drenched. His shoulder-length auburn hair hung in wet strips over his ears and forehead. His blue eyes gleamed with excitement.

Belle had inspired Maurice's latest invention: a steam balloon. She'd told her father about a novel she'd read in which the heroes traveled the world in a hot-air balloon. Although the book didn't explain *how* the machine worked, she knew there was no stopping her father from trying to figure it out.

"I almost forgot the best part!" Maurice said. "Tell her, Your Highness!"

The Prince rapped the side of the boiler with his hammer and grinned. "The Magic Stone works!"

The Magic Stone had been Belle's idea. The Prince had gotten it from an Enchantress, along

with a Magic Mirror and a Magic Atlas. The same Enchantress had put a spell on the Prince that turned him into a Beast, until Belle had come along and broken it.

The Magic Stone was a glowing rock that remained fiery hot, no matter how chilly the temperature. It had helped to keep the castle warm during the kingdom's cold winters. When the steam balloon needed a lightweight energy source to heat the clouds, the Stone seemed like the perfect solution.

"You were right," Maurice told Belle. "It's exactly hot enough to turn the water into steam, but not so hot that it causes the water to boil away too quickly. As long as there are clouds, the balloon could fly forever!"

"And as long as you can prevent the balloon from blowing up before it gets off the ground," Belle said. She picked up Maurice's blueprint for the steam balloon and studied it. She'd learned a

lot working at her father's side and was good at making the adjustments needed for his plans to work.

"Can I see?" Chip ran over to join Belle, who lowered the blueprint so he could look at it. "How does it work?" he asked.

Maurice pointed out the parts. "The suction valve draws in the clouds, which become water and flow into the tank. The Magic Stone heats the water and turns it into steam, which rises and fills the giant silk balloon. That keeps you flying. A pull cord opens a flap at the top of the balloon, to let steam escape so you can come back down to earth."

"Wow!" Chip said. "It's like something out of a book!"

Belle and Maurice exchanged a smile. "It's *exactly* like that," Belle said.

"How come it exploded, though?" Chip asked.

"I haven't quite figured that out," Maurice said.

Belle examined the boiler, which was easy to do with one side blown off. She studied each part, using her imagination to picture the boiler working. She mentally followed the steam as it rose through the pipes. . . .

"I've found the problem," Belle told her father. "You need more space between the steam valve and the ceiling of the boiler."

The Prince looked at Belle in surprise.

"Did you forget I used to be my father's chief assistant? Until *you* stole my job," Belle teased him.

"It looks like we need you back," the Prince replied. "Unless you're too busy with the village library."

"I can do both," Belle said—and she could. But a tiny part of her wished she could do more. Ever since she was a little girl, Belle had dreamed of traveling to faraway cities and exploring the world. While she loved working with her father and overseeing the library, she still craved adventure.

"Look, Belle! A toy pirate ship!" Chip held up a carved wooden ship with a tiny Jolly Roger flag attached to one mast.

"Take anything you like," the Prince told Chip. As Chip continued sorting through the toys, Belle, Maurice, and the Prince went to work repairing the boiler.

Just as they were finishing, tinkling music sounded from across the room. It was coming from a box in Chip's hands. The Prince turned and walked toward Chip, taking slow, deliberate steps, as if mesmerized.

"The music box . . . ," he said.

Chip held it out to him, but the Prince's arms remained at his sides. Curious, Belle took the box from Chip. It was made of ebony and inlaid with gold and silver geometric designs. Inside, a silver angel pirouetted on a spindle at the center of the box.

"It's beautiful," Belle said.

The Prince snatched it from Belle, his eyes flashing. "It's not mine." His voice was low, with a hint of his former beastly growl. "It belonged to my mother. I haven't seen it in years."

A moment later, his shoulders slumped. When he spoke again, it was in a whisper. "I'd forgotten all about it. . . ." The music slowed to its last few *plink plink plink*s and the angel stopped turning. "*No*. I didn't forget. . . ." He closed the lid. "I buried it away."

"I understand," Belle said gently. "I know what it's like to miss—"

"You don't understand at all!" Before Belle could respond, the Prince stormed out of the room, taking the music box with him.

"Did I do something wrong?" Chip asked, his eyes wide with worry.

"Of course not." Belle patted Chip's shoulder. "He'll be fine."

"Belle's right," Maurice said. "He just needs

time alone. He'll be back to his cheerful self by dinner, I'm sure."

Belle nodded. "He'll definitely be fine," she said. She hoped that by repeating the words, she would convince herself as well.

CHAPTER 2

The Prince didn't come down to dinner, however. He stayed locked in his sitting room all night and into the next day. Mrs. Potts had Lumiere, the castle's maître d', deliver the Prince's breakfast to his room the next morning—but Lumiere soon returned with the meal uneaten on the tray.

"He says he is not hungry," Lumiere told Belle when he returned to the kitchen. "And I think he

growled at me." He set down the tray and flipped his ponytail over his shoulder. "We should have left the hay bed in there."

"Balderdash!" cried Mrs. Potts. She waved a spoon at Lumiere. "I hope you're not implying that the master is turning back into a beast."

Although the rail-thin Lumiere towered over the squat cook, he knew better than to make her angry. "I only meant, *ma chère* Mrs. Potts," he said quickly, "that at least he'd have a place to sleep, since he hasn't left that room."

"I don't think we need to worry yet," Belle reassured them. "Seeing the music box made him think of his mother, and it upset him. We just have to give him more time."

Belle headed to her father's workshop, having returned—temporarily—to being his chief assistant. The Prince would come out soon; she was sure of it. He was as excited about the steam balloon as Maurice was. There was

no way he'd be able to stay away for long.

When another day passed, however, and the Prince remained locked away in his sitting room, Belle began to worry. He had continued to refuse his meals, even after Mrs. Potts made potato stew, his favorite meal.

Belle decided they'd given the Prince enough time to come out on his own. She knocked on his door.

"I said I'm not hungry!" the Prince barked after Belle had knocked. Barked or . . . *growled*? Was Lumiere right after all? Had the Prince turned back into a beast?

"It's not Mrs. Potts. It's Belle," Belle said.

"Belle . . . just go away. Please."

"I'm not leaving. Let me in." She paused and waited, listening closely. "You know I'll stand out

here all night if I have to." Finally, she heard his footsteps, and a moment later the door opened.

Belle was relieved when the Prince, not the Beast, appeared in the doorway. He was still human, but he looked beastly all the same. His eyes were tired and sunken, and his clothes were a wrinkled mess.

The room was dark, lit only by a single candle next to the chair. Curtains covered the balcony doors, blocking the sunlight. The music box sat silently on the mantel above the cold fireplace.

The Prince returned to his chair by the hearth. Belle recognized the ornate hand mirror he placed on his lap. It was the Magic Mirror from the Enchantress. The Beast had used it to keep watch on the world outside his enchanted castle.

"What are you looking at?" she asked.

"Nothing," replied the Prince, placing both hands over the mirror.

"Please," Belle said. The Prince sighed and

lifted the mirror. Its silver frame glowed with an otherworldly light, tinged with green. Sparks of gold circled the rim as a small, desolate peasant village appeared in the glass. The sky above the village was gray, and the roads were muddy. Shacks made of dirt and hay sat hunched next to each other as if trying to keep warm. The outline of a castle stood in the distance, wrapped in ominous shadows.

"Where is this?" Belle asked. "Is it nearby?"

The Prince stared down at the village grimly. "It's a place I ruined."

"I don't understand. How could you have—"

The Prince turned the mirror facedown in his lap. "I was so selfish, Belle. I didn't care about anyone else. That's why the Enchantress cursed me."

"But you paid the price for all that," Belle said. "You've changed. That's why you were able to become the Prince again. You care about *me*."

The Prince shook his head. "I don't deserve to be this kingdom's prince. I don't deserve to be a prince at all."

Belle sat down across from him and reached out to take his hand. "Whatever you did, we'll fix it," she said. "We'll use the Magic Atlas and go there, together."

The Prince pulled his hand free. "The Magic Atlas can't take me back in time, and that's the only way I can fix things."

"I'm pretty good at solving problems," Belle insisted. "Didn't I figure out the problem with the steam balloon?" The Prince looked up at her. His eyes were still haunted, but Belle detected a glimmer of curiosity in them. "I can't help, though," she continued, "unless you tell me what happened. Does it have something to do with the music box?"

The Prince nodded. "All right," he said. "I'll tell you. Because if you *can* help, it would be—"

"Belle! Monsieur Maurice needs you!"

Chip leaned through the doorway, gesturing urgently. "He's trying to attach the basket to the boiling something-or-other, and he can't find the bolt to the hinge—or maybe it was the hinge to the bolt—but anyway, he says *you* know where it is."

"Tell him I'll be there in a minute," Belle said. Chip nodded and darted off.

"It's all right, Belle," the Prince said.

"Papa will wait," Belle said. "This is more important."

"No, go on," he insisted. "I just realized how hungry I am, and I'd rather tell you my story on a full stomach. Is there any potato stew left?"

Belle grinned. "Mrs. Potts saved some for you."

The Prince smiled. "Go help your father find the bolt, or the hinge, or the whatever. I'll eat lunch and meet you in the workshop."

Belle felt relieved as she headed to the East Wing. All signs of the Beast were gone. The Prince was back.

CHAPTER 3

"P_{apa!}"

Belle burst into the workshop to find her father bent awkwardly over the steam balloon. Chip tugged vainly on his waist.

"What happened?" She raced to the balloon. Her father's arm had gotten trapped between the balloon's boiler and a cedar basket that now stood

crookedly atop it. It was where the passengers would ride.

"I—uh—dropped—"

"Hold on, Papa." Belle slipped her hands under the bottom of the basket and used all her strength to lift it. Chip and Maurice fell backward as Maurice's arm was freed from its trap. Belle gently helped her father from the floor.

"I was lifting the basket onto the boiler," Maurice explained through gritted teeth. "But I didn't line it up right, and my arm got caught."

"You shouldn't have tried to do it alone, Papa."

"It's cedar! We chose that kind of wood because it's sturdy and *lightweight*."

"You still should have waited for me to help you." Belle could see the bruises already forming underneath her father's skin. His elbow was bent at an awkward angle. "You might have broken your elbow."

"Nonsense. It's just a little— *Ow!*"

21

He grabbed his elbow in pain.

Belle turned to Chip. "Ask Cogsworth to send for the doctor, please. Then go tell the Prince what happened."

Chip dashed out as Belle led her father to a chair. "Has the Prince come out?" Maurice asked. "Did you find out what happened to upset him?"

"I don't know all the details yet, but he's eating Mrs. Potts's stew, so that's a good sign."

Maurice waved a hand at Belle in a shooing motion. "Go on—finish breaking whatever new spell he's under. You don't have to stay here with me."

"I'm not going anywhere, Papa. Not until the doctor comes." Belle pulled up a chair next to her father. "The Prince is probably on his way here already."

The doctor arrived first. He examined Maurice's elbow and diagnosed a bad sprain. He then wrapped the arm and instructed Maurice to

avoid any further heavy lifting.

In the meantime, Chip returned and reported that when he'd arrived at the Prince's sitting room, the Prince wasn't there. Belle assumed this meant the Prince was on his way. But by the time the doctor left, the Prince had yet to appear.

Where was he?

Belle persuaded her father to take a nap and rest his arm. She then returned to the Prince's sitting room. Except for the absence of the Prince, everything appeared to be exactly as it was when she'd been there earlier.

The music box was still on the mantel, and the Magic Mirror was still on the Prince's chair. . . .

The Magic Mirror!

Belle hurried over and picked it up. As she did, Chip raced in with Mrs. Potts, Cogsworth,

and Lumiere. He had told them about the Prince's disappearance.

"Show me the Prince," Belle told the mirror.

The familiar green glow shimmered up the silver handle and around the frame. Her reflection disappeared and the mirror went black.

A moment later, a tall figure stumbled into view, pushed by someone else. The figure turned, revealing—

"The Prince!" Cogsworth cried.

Belle's heart dropped at the sight. Only hours earlier he'd been here, looking into the mirror with her, and now . . .

Two grim guards in iron helmets appeared. One of them swung shut a door made of thick iron bars, locking the Prince inside a dungeon cell.

"Where are you?" Belle whispered into the mirror. She knew the Prince couldn't hear her, yet he seemed to be looking right at her, his eyes haunted.

Behind the guards, in the shadows, appeared the silhouette of a woman in a long gown.

"A witch?" Lumiere asked, squinting closely.

"No . . . ," Belle said. The woman raised a candle she held in her hand. Light from the flame glinted off the jewels in her crown. "A queen."

The queen called out from the darkness, speaking in French. "I . . . will . . . *NEVER* . . . forgive you!"

She spun away, her gown swirling with an angry whoosh. Her shoes clacked against the stone floor as she disappeared from view.

The guards marched after her, the *thunk thunk thunk* of their boots echoing off the dungeon walls. The last sound was a distant *clang* as the cell door crashed closed.

Then . . . silence.

Belle watched the Prince slink to a corner. He slid to the floor, his slumped shoulders barely visible in the dim light coming through a barred window, high up in the cell wall.

Worry tightened around Belle's heart, making it difficult for her to breathe.

"I'll find you," she whispered into the mirror. "I'll find you and I'll rescue you. I promise."

CHAPTER 4

But how could Belle find the Prince? She was certain he'd gone to the kingdom he'd shown her in the mirror, but because she didn't know the kingdom's name, the mirror remained blank every time she asked it to show her where he was.

He had to be nearby, though. How else could he have gotten there so fast on foot?

Before Belle finished this thought, she knew

the answer. She raced downstairs to the royal library. She dashed to the mantel above the room's fireplace—but the Magic Atlas was gone. The Prince had used it to travel to the village in the mirror, which meant he could be miles and miles away.

Belle wasn't deterred. She found Cogsworth and Lumiere. "It seems likely he's in France, at least," she told them. "The queen we saw in the mirror spoke French, and she clearly knows the Prince and thinks he has wronged her somehow." They sat down in front of a large map of the country and got to work.

Cogsworth read off the cities and kingdoms one by one. Belle commanded the Magic Mirror to show her each place Cogsworth named, looking for any resemblance to the village the Prince had shown her.

"Hearing the names of all these places reminds me of the journeys I took as a child with my

parents," said Lumiere. "We were troubadours, you know, and performed for crowds throughout the country."

"Maybe you visited the village where the Prince is being held!" Belle cried.

Lumiere's brow furrowed in concentration. "*Je suis très desolé,* Belle," he said, shaking his head. "I'm very sorry. I was so young then. I hardly even remember their names."

They resumed their search, and as the evening went deep into the night, Belle became more and more frustrated. Magic wasn't going to help her locate the Prince. She would have to figure out another way.

She had an idea where to start....

Belle sat in the Prince's chair, the music box in her hands. She held it up and studied it from every

angle. The delicately painted designs were even more beautiful up close.

The music box was the only other clue Belle had to the Prince's disappearance. She was certain it had triggered his vision of the mysterious village in the mirror, but as much as she tried, she couldn't decipher any meaning in its intricate geometric patterns.

She opened the lid of the box, and the silver angel popped up. Belle wound the key on the side of the box, and music began to play. The angel spun on her spindle as the box tinkled its short, pretty tune. The music was haunting this late at night.

Belle set the box down and picked up the Magic Mirror. "Show me the Prince," she instructed the mirror.

The Prince's hunched figure appeared in the same bleak cell. A faint thread of moonlight shone through the bars of the window. Through

it, a pair of jagged mountain peaks rose from the dark horizon.

"Tell me where you are," Belle begged in a desperate whisper. *"Please."* But the Prince remained unmoving and silent. The music box's song slowed, then stopped, and the mirror went dark once more.

CHAPTER 5

"I've brought you some tea, my dear! And a plate of scones, fresh from the oven."

At the sound of Mrs. Potts's voice, Belle opened her eyes to find the morning sun streaming in through the window. She had fallen asleep! She leapt from the chair without thinking, and—

CRASH!

The Magic Mirror slid to the marble floor.

"No!" Belle cried. She snatched up the mirror. Shards of silver clung to its frame, while the rest of the glass lay on the floor in a pile of jagged pieces. "It's shattered." Her voice was choked with despair.

"I'm so sorry!" Mrs. Potts helped Belle carefully collect the pieces. "This is my fault!"

"It's all right, Mrs. Potts," Belle reassured her.

Mrs. Potts handed a large shard of the broken mirror to Belle. "Maybe the magic isn't gone," she said.

"Show me the Prince," Belle said to the shard. But the mirror displayed only her disappointed face.

"We could glue it back together," Mrs. Potts said hopefully.

Belle doubted this would work. She reached down to pick up the last piece of the broken mirror—and a beam of light hit her eyes.

The sun was bouncing off the glittery painted

design on top of the music box, sending a rainbow of light into the room. Belle set down the mirror and picked up the box.

"This all started when the Prince found this music box," Belle told Mrs. Potts. "But I can't figure out how it's connected to his disappearance."

"Ah, yes," Mrs. Potts said with a knowing nod. "That's the music box Queen Adele—the Prince's mother—received from her sister, Cecile."

"She had a sister?"

Mrs. Potts nodded. "A twin. They were as close as two peas, as the saying goes." She made room on the tea tray for the broken mirror pieces. "I'd just started as a scullery maid when the queen's sister got married and moved away."

Belle studied the music box. "Does the Prince know the box came from his aunt?"

"I couldn't say, dear," Mrs. Potts replied. "The Prince wasn't yet born when his aunt Cecile left and became a queen herself, thanks to the king she

married. What I *do* remember is that the Prince's mother was very sad to be separated from her twin. Queen Cecile's new kingdom was miles away, you see. Not long after she left, she sent Queen Adele this music box. It plays the sisters' favorite tune, one they sang when they were girls."

Belle wound up the music box and opened the lid. The angel spun to the tinkling melody.

"Pretty, isn't it? I'd often hear it echoing down the castle's hallways. Queen Adele would play it and look forward to the day she would visit Queen Cecile and introduce the Prince to his aunt and uncle." Mrs. Potts shook her head with a wistful sigh. "Alas, our queen died before the visit could happen. The two sisters never saw each other again."

When Belle considered the music box, the kingdom in the mirror, and the twin queens, there was only one explanation that made sense: the kingdom in the mirror had to be where the Prince's

aunt Cecile lived. Belle was sure of it.

"Could the queen we saw in the Magic Mirror last night be the Prince's aunt?" Belle asked Mrs. Potts.

"Oh, no. The Prince's aunt Cecile died a few years ago."

Belle felt a pang of grief on behalf of the Prince. He'd suffered more than she realized. She remained certain there was a link, though, between the Prince's aunt and his imprisonment.

"What was the name of the aunt's kingdom?" she asked Mrs. Potts.

Mrs. Potts thought a moment. "It was south of here, I believe. Broomo, or maybe Bambou? Oh! Wait just a moment." She hurried off and came back a few moments later carrying a large canvas. "I'd nearly forgotten about this. Queen Cecile sent it along with the music box."

Belle helped Mrs. Potts set the canvas down. It was a painting of an elegant royal couple—a queen

seated on a throne, a king standing behind her, his hand on her shoulder.

"This is Queen Cecile's wedding portrait," Mrs. Potts explained. Belle noticed the similarities between Queen Cecile and the images she'd seen of Queen Adele in paintings around the castle. "She was beautiful." Mrs. Potts sighed. "Just like her sister."

Belle agreed. Like his mother, the Prince's aunt had auburn hair and blue eyes. There was tenderness in Queen Cecile's expression, and warmth. The king had dark features, his hair and eyes a brown so deep they were almost black. He, too, radiated compassion.

Mrs. Potts pointed to an inscription at the bottom of the painting: *Le nouveau roi et la nouvelle reine de Brumeux.* "See? 'Broomo.'"

Belle realized the cook's Irish accent had led her to mispronounce Brumeux as "*Broom*-oh." Not that it mattered. When Belle returned to the map,

neither Brumeux nor Broomo were on it.

"Are you sure it was in France?" Belle asked.

"It's the one thing I remember for sure," Mrs. Potts insisted. "The Prince's mother always said they might have to cross mountains to visit each other, but at least they wouldn't have to cross borders. Although, as I told you, the visit never happened."

"Here you go!" Cogsworth swept into the room, the Magic Mirror in his hand. Mrs. Potts had asked him to fix it. "Good as new!" he announced.

The pieces of the mirror had been glued into place, but the surface was still cracked, skewing Belle's reflection and making it appear as though her eyes were above each other instead of side by side. She wasn't surprised when she asked the mirror to show her the Prince and nothing happened. The Magic Mirror was just a mirror now—a *broken* one.

"Thank you for trying," she told Cogsworth.

Lumiere entered the library behind Cogsworth. "If you had let *me* do it—" He caught sight of the painting. *"Les Collines Flous!"* He pointed to the cloudy mountain peaks in the corner of the painting. "These mountains. These are *Les Collines Flous.*"

Cogsworth snorted. "Who'd name a mountain range the Fuzzy Hills? It's ridiculous!"

"That's why I remember the name," insisted Lumiere. "Because it was so foggy there. It was a rare day when the sun could push its way through before it set. My parents and I performed in a little village at the base of the mountains."

Belle peered at the peaks more closely. There was something familiar about them. "Was the kingdom named Brumeux?" she asked Lumiere.

"Oui! I believe so!" replied Lumiere. *"Brumeux—* 'misty.' And the village was Brumeuxville."

"I saw those mountains through the window of the Prince's cell," Belle told the group. "They had

jagged points, just like in the painting."

She returned to the map, running her finger along the southern border. "I've found it!" She pointed to where the words *Les Collines Flous* could be seen in tiny print, curved over a pair of lightly sketched peaks.

Belle smiled in relief. She'd found the Prince.

CHAPTER 6

It would take days to get to Brumeux by carriage. But the steam balloon could travel there in less than a day—if they could get it to fly.

As soon as Belle told her father what she had learned, they went back to work. They tested every part of the balloon several times. There were no more explosions. Everything worked just

as it was supposed to. The balloon was ready.

At dawn the next morning, two stable hands carried the balloon up to the roof of the East Wing and set it down gently. The cedar basket was now firmly attached, and the giant silk balloon cascaded over the side, waiting to be filled.

"You remembered to pack the compass?" Maurice asked Belle. "And the telescope?"

"Yes, Papa," Belle assured her father. She climbed up a short ladder and stepped into the cedar basket. "They're in the cabinet with the other tools."

She pointed to the small box Maurice had installed in a wall of the basket.

"And the map?"

"I have it right here." She patted the front pocket of her dress.

The stable hands filled the engine's tank with water to give them enough power to lift off until they could reach the clouds. Belle could feel the

Magic Stone heating the water, warming the wood beneath her feet.

"I just realized there's no protection from lightning!" Maurice exclaimed worriedly. "Or what if there's a blizzard?"

"It's spring, Papa, and we're going south," Belle said. "I promise I won't fly into any thunderstorms. I haven't forgotten what you told me: once we're up, we only need to find enough clouds to supplement our wind power." She smiled. "I'll make sure we only go near 'happy' clouds."

Maurice frowned. "I still think I should come with you."

"Papa. We already decided—not with your sprained elbow."

"You've never flown a balloon before, Belle! Much less a steam balloon all alone."

"She won't be alone, *mon cher* Maurice!" Lumiere glided through the arched stone doorway that framed the top of the East Wing staircase. "She

43

will be accompanied by the most responsible and trustworthy member of this household!" He took a bow.

"Thank heaven for that!" Cogsworth said as he appeared behind Lumiere, a picnic basket over his arm. "Belle would be doomed before she started if it were just *you* going with her." He turned to Maurice. "Rest assured, Belle will be in the best of hands." He flipped open the top of the picnic basket and drew back the red-and-white-checked cloth inside. "As instructed, by *me*, Mrs. Potts has packed the most lightweight of meals. We have a loaf of bread, two hunks of Swiss cheese—the holes make it extra light—and a tin of dried apple slices."

Belle reached down to take the picnic basket from Cogsworth.

"Freshly baked biscuits, piping hot from the oven!" Mrs. Potts emerged from the archway with Chip, holding a cotton-wrapped bundle. She passed it up to Belle.

"Thank you," Belle said.

Maurice licked his finger and held it up. "Wind is in the southwesterly direction," he said. "Plenty of moisture in the air, which means a near-guaranteed chance of—"

"Clouds!" Chip shouted, eagerly pointing to the sky over the West Wing towers, where a giant snow-white cloudbank drifted toward them. The clouds picked up speed, and a moment later, a sudden sharp wind rustled the open end of the balloon.

"Grab it!" Maurice shouted. The stable hands reached out to snatch the ropes that connected the balloon to the cedar basket, but the silk panels had already filled with air. They poufed out, and the balloon began rising, yanking the ropes out of the stable hands' grip.

The boiler bounced along the stones, and Belle was thrown against the side of the basket. The excitement she'd felt earlier transformed into

terror, and she was seized with dread that she'd be making the journey alone.

Belle hung on to the edge of the basket and watched as Lumiere and Cogsworth raced after the escaping balloon. Lumiere scrambled up the side ladder, diving over the rim and dropping to the floor at Belle's feet. Belle held her hand out to Cogsworth, who huffed after the balloon and tried to leap inside. But between his short height and generous weight, he barely got off the ground.

"Lumiere!" Belle yelled. Lumiere quickly stood and stretched over the edge of the basket. He grabbed Cogsworth's meaty arms and yanked him up with a grunt. Belle grabbed Cogsworth's jacket, and together she and Lumiere hauled Cogsworth into the balloon.

"Don't worry!" Belle called down to Maurice as the balloon rose over the wall. "We'll be all right!"

The cloud bank was overhead now. The wind grew stronger.

"Hold on!" Belle yelled to her companions as the wind blew the balloon roughly forward, causing the basket to sway. Belle watched her father and the others at the top of the tower grow smaller as the balloon gathered speed, still rocking violently.

Apparently, even "happy" clouds weren't safe.

CHAPTER 7

Belle clutched the side of the basket and tried to wave to the tiny figures at the top of the castle, but the balloon continued to sway, and she needed both hands to keep from losing her balance. The door to the tool cabinet broke open, and the tools, along with the telescope and the compass, fell out and slipped through the slats in the floor before

Belle could reach for them, clanking against the boiler as they tumbled to the earth below.

Lumiere gripped one of the balloon's ropes and was thrown about by gusts of wind that seemed to come from every direction. Cogsworth appeared relatively safe, at least, curled up in a ball in a corner of the basket.

"What is that?" Cogsworth whimpered as a tinny clatter sounded from the bottom of the boiler. Belle peered out and discovered that they were scraping the top of the forest's trees.

"Are we falling?" cried Lumiere.

"I think I'm going to be ill," Cogsworth moaned. He clutched his stomach. "Correction: I *am* ill."

Belle felt a stab of panic but tried to ignore it. "We just need to get steam into the balloon," she called over the wind. She made her way along the basket rim to the rod that controlled the steam. When she turned it toward her, a tiny puff of hot air coughed its way up from the boiler.

"I see it!" Lumiere yelled in relief, watching the steam swirl upward. But it wasn't strong or steady enough yet to reach the balloon, which still flapped violently above them.

"The steam is blowing away instead of blowing straight up!" Belle shouted. The balloon lurched, sending the picnic basket skittering across the bottom. It bonked Cogsworth in the head.

"*Ow!*" Cogsworth moaned. "I *knew* this was a ridiculous scheme." He rubbed his scalp. "Your father is a madman, Belle—no offense. How could anyone believe a *steam* balloon could work?"

"It *does* work," Belle insisted. "And it *will*." She was terrified Cogsworth might be right, but her fear made her even more determined not to give up. "There should be more steam soon. Help me pull the balloon to the middle. We have to be ready when the boiler's at full power."

Belle and Lumiere used all their strength to tug the open end of the silk balloon over the top

of the large tin cylinder in the center of the cedar basket. That was where the steam would come out. Beneath them, the boiler chugged and vibrated. "Cogsworth! Turn the rod when I tell you!" Belle called out.

Cogsworth crawled to the steam-valve rod and clutched the base with both hands.

"Ready!" Belle yelled to Cogsworth, who shut his eyes tight and twisted his wrists. The rod turned, the valve opened, and steam burst out. Belle could feel it warming her hands as it filled the balloon, inflating the silk panels until they were stretched as wide and high as they could go.

The balloon began to rise, up, up, up, above the forest and into the clear blue sky. Belle exhaled a huge sigh of relief.

"We did it!" Lumiere said. He hugged Belle, then realized that he'd let go of the ropes and quickly reached out to grab them again.

"It's all right," Belle said. "I think you can let go now."

The wind had calmed, and the balloon had stopped swaying. Belle stepped over to Cogsworth. His knuckles were white from his grip on the rod. His face was just as pale, his eyes still tightly closed. "We can turn off the steam," she told him gently. They weren't just above the forest now; they were beyond it. The balloon glided smoothly forward. "It's safe to get up. I promise."

"*Oui, mon ami,*" Lumiere said. "No need to be afraid. Everything's fine. *Un peu* of a rocky start, that's all."

Cogsworth squinted one eye. "I'm actually quite comfortable down here," he said, trying to keep the tremor out of his voice. "This way, I can keep a close watch on our lunch." He hugged the picnic basket to his chest.

Belle joined Lumiere at the edge of the balloon's basket and gazed at the countryside below. Striped

swatches of farmland alternated with green fields and meadows dotted with color. It was like a giant patchwork quilt, spread out so far and wide it seemed to go on forever.

"Comme c'est belle!" Lumiere sighed.

"It is," Belle agreed. "Beautiful." Here and there was a tiny rectangle or square of a house or barn. The ovals and ribbons of the lakes and rivers were as blue as the sky.

"You are missing it, *mon ami!*" Lumiere called down to Cogsworth. Belle glanced over her shoulder, relieved to see that Cogsworth was sitting up, and the pink had returned to his cheeks.

"I'll join you in just a minute," he replied. He began to stand up, but a flicker of fear flashed across his face and he sat back down. "Perhaps two."

Lumiere looked at Belle and shrugged.

Belle felt a breeze blow past her shoulder. "The wind's changed direction," she said. "We need

to rise farther or we'll be blown back the way we came."

"How will rising help?" Lumiere asked.

"The wind moves in different directions at different altitudes," Belle explained. "That's how birds fly where they want to go—they rise until they reach the right current."

Belle crossed to the steam rod to open it but hesitated. She glanced at Cogsworth and then turned to Lumiere. "Would you like to open the valve this time?" she asked him.

"*Ah, oui! Bien sûr!*" Lumiere darted to Belle's side.

"No, no, no!" Cogsworth protested. "That's *my* job!" As Belle had hoped, he was energized by the possibility of Lumiere's outdoing him. He burst off the floor and thrust out a hand to clasp the rod.

"Are you ready?" Belle asked. Cogsworth nodded. "Go ahead."

Cogsworth drew the handle toward him. A

moment later, steam emerged and the balloon rose.

"Keep it open until I tell you," Belle instructed. She closed her eyes, waiting. She didn't have feathers for the breeze to ruffle or wings to sense the current, but she could still feel the wind on her cheeks and through her hair. It made a hushing sound that blew against one ear and brushed across her face. After a few minutes, it changed. It now whispered in her other ear, grazing her face from the other direction. "That's enough!" Belle opened her eyes. "You can turn it off."

"Done!" Cogsworth announced proudly. He put his free hand on his hip, as if posing for a portrait.

"Thank you," Belle said. "That was perfect." She gave Lumiere a pointed look and nodded in Cogsworth's direction.

"*Oui, oui,*" Lumiere said reluctantly, getting the hint. "*Magnifique,*" he added with the slightest roll of his eyes.

Cogsworth beamed, pleased. "Consider me the balloon's official steam releaser." He drew out his pocket watch and peered down at it. "Nearly noon!" he reported brightly. "Time for lunch."

Belle smiled, happy that Cogsworth's fear had fled at last.

They set out their food on a shelf below the basket's ledge, to protect it from the wind. They were quiet as they ate, taking in the view. The clouds grew sparser the farther they traveled, but the wind remained unchanging, carrying them steadily southward.

Finally, clouds appeared again, a misty gray mass that spread along the horizon.

"Ah!" Lumiere cried. "Right in our path! As if waiting for us to absorb them."

"That's not *only* clouds," Belle said. As they sailed closer, the wide stone wall of a kingdom emerged from the mist.

"Brumeux?" Lumiere asked.

Belle shook her head. "I don't think so," she said. "Could we have traveled that far south so quickly?" She withdrew the map from her pocket and unfolded it. "If I can find this kingdom on the map, it'll tell us how far we've come and how far we still need to go."

"In the meantime, we can capture those clouds!" Lumiere declared. "I shall stand by!" He took his place at the crank that worked the suction valve, which would pull in the clouds.

"We need to raise the balloon first," warned Belle. "We don't want to hit the wall."

"Step aside, Lumiere." Cogsworth elbowed Lumiere away so he could grab the steam-valve rod. "Say the word, mademoiselle!"

"Go ahead," Belle told Cogsworth. He opened the steam-valve, and the balloon rose.

"I think this is the lake we passed not too long ago," Belle said, running her finger down the map. "But I don't see a kingdom nearby." She hoped

they hadn't gotten off track somehow.

"Allow me," Cogsworth said. Belle handed him the map.

"I have traveled the country, remember," Lumiere said. "*I* should look." He plucked the map from Cogsworth's hand. Cogsworth snatched it back. Lumiere lunged for it again, but as he did, a breeze blew by and the map flew out of Cogsworth's hand. *"Mon Dieu!"* Lumiere cried.

Belle reached for the map, but it whisked past her, grazing her fingers before sailing off on the breeze.

"How *could* you?" Cogsworth said to Lumiere.

"It was an accident!" Lumiere protested.

A loud *bong* broke through their arguing. "Never mind the map!" Belle shouted, staring ahead in horror.

A clock tower, which had been hidden by the clouds, clearly poked up from behind the fast-approaching wall. "We need to rise," Belle told the

others, "or we'll run into that tower!" Another *bong* sounded, like a warning.

The balloon flew closer, and Belle could see the spires of a large castle beyond the tower. She dashed to the steam rod and pulled it toward her. All that came out was a gurgle. Belle jiggled the rod. A cough, then another gurgle. The pipes in the boiler below them let out a loud *clank*.

"Is that a bad sound?" Cogsworth asked, clutching Lumiere's arm.

"Mais non," insisted Lumiere. "We're fine." His tone was calm, but he held tight to Cogsworth. "Right, Belle?"

The clock tower chimed again. *Bong!*

Belle didn't respond. She was certain her friends knew the answer.

Bong!

The balloon was sinking. . . .

Bong!

They were out of steam.

CHAPTER 8

C*RASH!*

The balloon's boiler smashed into the top of the kingdom's wall, knocking loose several stones. Belle heard a clatter as the stones landed somewhere below. The collision threw them out of the path of the clock tower, but they were still in danger of crashing into the castle. They needed

60

steam, which meant they needed clouds. Luckily, they were surrounded by clouds.

While Cogsworth and Lumiere huddled in fright, Belle grabbed the suction crank and pumped it with one hand, drawing in the clouds. She used her other hand to twist the steam rod to keep the valve open.

She heard a faint rattle as the Magic Stone warmed the clouds and the vapor began to make its way through the boiler pipes.

The sound snapped Lumiere out of his frightened daze. "We need to fuel the tank!" he shouted. He rushed to Belle's side.

"Yes, yes!" Cogsworth cried, hurrying to join them. "This is no time to panic! We must take action!" He clutched the steam rod while Belle and Lumiere worked together to pump in clouds from the mist around them.

The balloon's direction shifted and they narrowly slid past the castle. Belle could see the

structure's tallest spire just outside the rim of the basket. The castle grew smaller as the balloon rose higher. No light shone from any of the castle windows. Dark and gloomy, it was like a walled-off ruin, desolate and forgotten.

The balloon caught a current and carried them forward. The castle vanished into the fog behind them. Even more fog was in front of them, making it impossible to see what lay ahead.

Cogsworth narrowed his eyes at their murky surroundings. "Awfully dark all of a sudden," he observed.

"We have been traveling through clouds, *mon ami*," Lumiere said. "Which means we cannot see the sun—this is why it is dark. It is as obvious as the nose on your face. In fact ..." He pointed to a strip of mist floating past. "There is a cloud *on* your face!" He laughed. Cogsworth frowned.

Belle glanced around. Cogsworth was right. It *had* gotten darker—and it seemed to be growing

darker every second. It looked like it did when it was about to—

"Rain!" Lumiere held his hand out, palm up.

Belle leaned back so that the silk globe above them no longer shielded her face. Cool drops fell on her cheeks and forehead.

"Aha! I was right—*again!*" Cogsworth blinked as raindrops landed on his eyelids. It was only a sprinkle, though, and it stopped almost as soon as it started.

"That wasn't *too* bad," Lumiere pronounced, brushing the raindrops off his sleeves. "*Très* refreshing, in fact!"

Belle had a clear view of the sky above her, however, and her heart skipped a beat at what she saw. "I don't think it's over," she told Cogsworth and Lumiere. Far above, a large black mass roiled and churned with an angry energy.

"If we go lower, maybe we can catch a faster current." Belle grabbed the pull cord to release

some steam. "Yell if you see trees or towers, or anything else we need to steer around."

"I see nothing," Cogsworth reported.

"Literally . . . *rien*—nothing," Lumiere echoed.

"We should look for a safe place to land until the sky clears again," said Belle. Unfortunately, the ground was covered in the same mist that had buried the castle, making it impossible to see what was beneath them. It could be an open field or a village of densely packed houses.

Suddenly, a strange rumble came from the sky. A blinding light exploded at the middle of the dark cloud, followed by a deafening roar.

"It's alive!" Lumiere shouted.

The storm cloud let out a peeved *snap* in answer and set off another flash of light. A second later, raindrops flooded down, as if a dam had suddenly burst.

The balloon skidded over the top of a grove of trees. Branches scraped the bottom of the boiler.

A bewildered blue songbird, startled from its nest, fluttered past Belle's nose, chirping.

Belle turned the rod to release more steam, and the balloon rose. The downpour became a drizzle, and Belle was relieved to see the black cloud sail beyond them, taking the rain with it. There were a few puddles on the floor of the cedar basket, but most of the water had drained away.

The sky remained gray as they sailed forward, and a fine mist hung in the air. A few outlines of straw-covered shacks were visible through the fog below.

Lumiere wrung the water from his ponytail. "I remember a performance we gave in one village," he said. "We were right in the middle of our finale, when—*whoosh!* A downpour just like this one. *Quelle surprise!* It stopped almost as soon as it started, so we shook off the rain and finished our song." He chuckled. "My father always said *'Le spectacle doit continuer!'* The show must go on."

He flicked his ponytail over his shoulder, then paused, thoughtful. "I believe that village . . ." He leaned out over the basket and squinted ahead. "It was! Brumeuxville!" He pointed into the dewy distance. "And there are *Les Collines Flous!*"

Belle joined Lumiere and squinted into the mist. At first, the vista ahead looked merely like shades of gray to her. Soon, however, the fog thinned, revealing two jagged peaks on the horizon—two *very* familiar jagged peaks.

"We're here!" Belle shouted. She hugged Lumiere. "The Prince must be in the castle we passed over!" She was overcome with emotion—joy, relief, and eagerness to see the Prince. Tears came to her eyes, but she wiped them away, as she had the raindrops. "Now we just need to find a place to land." She peered over the side of the basket, looking for a break in the fog that would allow a clear view of what lay below.

The chirping she'd heard moments before grew

louder, and the blue songbird appeared out of the gray. Belle followed its path with her eyes, hoping the bird might lead them to a clearing. Instead, the bird swooped up toward the top of the balloon and was soon out of sight.

"I think I see something," Cogsworth said, gesturing ahead.

Belle saw it, too—a large patch of green and yellow. It could be a pasture or a farm plot, but either way, it seemed like the safest place to set down. "As soon as we're close enough, I'll let out the steam," she said. As Belle took the pull cord in her hand, she heard an odd *pop* above them, followed by a loud hiss. A second later, a small shape fell past her face. She instinctively reached out to catch it, and the blue songbird landed in her open palms. Its tiny eyes blinked rapidly. On the end of its beak was a tiny scrap of silk.

The hissing grew louder. Above them, the balloon deflated, shrinking from a large orb to

a giant wrinkled sock. The weight of the boiler pulled the balloon toward the ground too fast for Lumiere and Cogsworth to have time to scream, too fast for Belle to let go of the bird, and too fast for her to think of anything they could do to stop them from—

CRASH!

CHAPTER
9

Everything was dark. Dark and ... and *silky*. Belle raised her arms, and her fingers poked into fabric. She was lying faceup underneath a silk panel of the balloon.

"Lumiere?" she called, her voice muffled by the fabric. "Cogsworth?" The ground beneath her was lumpy and prickly. Her dress was covered with

69

mud and dried grass. She ran her fingers through her hair: more mud and straw. Her right shoulder ached and she felt a small scrape on her cheek, but she wasn't bleeding and didn't seem to be seriously injured. They'd all been thrown free of the basket, and the giant silk balloon must have floated down on top of them. Judging from what she could see around her, they'd landed in a hayfield.

She called again for her friends. There was no reply except for a tiny *cheep* next to her leg. The bird! Had she crushed it? Another muffled *cheep*. Belle spotted the blue songbird, wrapped in the twisted folds of the fabric. She scooped it up, and the bird cried out in alarm: *Cheep!* She noticed that one of its wings was crooked.

There was a moan from somewhere nearby. Belle gently set the bird down in some hay. "I'll be right back," she promised. She crawled in the direction of the moaning. "Cogsworth? Lumiere?"

"Here!" A gangly body sat up from the ground

like a mummy, blue silk wrapped around its head. "I can't get out!" Lumiere's hands tugged at the fabric.

"Stay still a minute," Belle said. She gently unwrapped the silk.

His ponytail had become loose, and strands of hair hung in his eyes. He brushed them away and looked around. "We're alive!" He paused for a moment, worried. "Aren't we?"

Before Belle could answer, there was another moan, louder than before. *"Ooooooh."*

"Cogsworth!" Belle shouted. "Where are you?"

"Aaaaagh!"

Belle saw a ripple flutter through the silk. She and Lumiere approached on hands and knees and found Cogsworth on his stomach, writhing. "My foot!" he cried. "It's gone!" He gestured toward his feet.

Belle and Lumiere crawled toward Cogsworth's ankles and discovered something large and heavy

weighing down the silk on top of his foot.

"Part of the steam balloon must have landed on it," Belle said.

Cogsworth craned his neck to see. "It's crushed!" he shrieked. "As good as gone!"

"Don't worry. We'll get it off," Belle told him. She nodded to Lumiere, who heaved the silk-wrapped object with a grunt. Belle pulled Cogsworth's leg free as he let out another pained groan.

Belle bent down to inspect his foot. "It isn't crushed," she said. "But it *is* swollen. It might be sprained or broken."

"I'll never walk again!" Cogsworth whined.

"I'm sure you will," Belle reassured him. "We'll find a doctor in the village." She stood, pushing the silk up over her head with her hands. "We just need to find the edge of this so we can get out—"

"Hey! Who's under there?" called a gravelly voice. "Are you some kind of monster invaders from the sky?"

"Hello?" Belle called back in her friendliest tone. "Can you help us? We've—"

"Quiet! I'll tell you when you can speak, monsters."

"But you just asked us—" began Lumiere.

"Quiet, I said!" This time the voice was higher, but it soon lowered again. "I'm a mighty soldier, and I've got a sword! I'm not afraid to use it, either!" A sharp point poked into the fabric near Belle. The songbird, near Belle's feet, let out a fearful *cheep*.

"Be careful!" Belle warned. "You'll hit the bird!"

"Bird?" This time the voice was unmistakably higher. It was *not* the sound of a mighty soldier—at least, not a grown-up one. "I mean," the stranger said, the voice even lower than before, "*what* bird?"

"It's a songbird," Belle answered. "It's injured." She was now pretty sure it was a child they were talking to—a child trying hard to sound like an adult. "It hurt its wing when we fell. I'll show you." She scooped the bird from the hay and lifted the

edge of the silk balloon over her head, stepping out into the foggy gray day.

Belle looked around for the mighty soldier, but the drizzle falling from the sky got in her eyes and made it difficult to see. She wiped the drops from her eyelids, blinked, and was finally able to make out a dark shape in the fog. A *short* dark shape, about up to her waist.

Her suspicion had been right. It was a child—a girl, about eight or nine years old. She wore a dress made of heavy burlap, decorated with hand-sewn stars. The girl's damp, sandy hair hung in uneven chunks around her narrow, freckled face. At the sight of the bird, now cupped in both of Belle's palms, the girl's fierce scowl softened and her dark eyes grew big. The bird fluttered the raindrops from its good wing and cheeped.

"*Aw,*" cooed the girl.

Belle smiled. "*Bonjour.*" She held out the bird. "Would you like—"

The girl growled and raised her "sword," a crooked branch nearly as long as she was tall. "Don't you try to 'good day' me, Mademoiselle Monster from the Sky! How do I know that 'bird' isn't some dragon you've worked your evil magic on?" The girl waved the heavy branch, throwing herself off-balance. She quickly grabbed it in both hands and planted it in the ground to steady herself. "If you want to invade my village, you'll have to fight me first!" She yanked the branch up and stabbed it into the mud again for emphasis.

"We're not monsters, I promise," Belle said. "We're people, like you. We're from a village north of here. My father built the balloon we flew here in. That's why you saw us come out of the sky. It wasn't magic. Well . . . mostly not."

She glanced around. Shards of wood and hunks of metal were scattered as far as she could see into the fog. The basket had clearly shattered when they hit the ground, and the boiler had been

wrenched apart. She searched for the orange glow of the Magic Stone, but there wasn't even a glimmer of it in the murky gray surrounding them.

"We're not invaders, either," Belle continued. "We need help." Another muffled groan from Cogsworth rose from under the balloon. "One of my friends hurt his ankle," she told the girl. "If you could take us to a doctor—"

"How many of you *are* there?" The girl's eyes flashed. "I'll fight an army if I have to!"

"No army," Belle said. "Just me and my two friends, Lumiere and Cogsworth. And this little fellow." She stepped forward and again held the bird out to the girl.

The girl instinctively took the bird in her palms, forgetting her branch, which remained upright next to her, stuck in the mud. "Aw, poor thing," she whispered. She gently stroked its tiny head with her finger. "You'll be all right. Granny T will fix you all up."

"Would you like to meet my friends?" Belle asked. Before the girl could reply, Belle called over her shoulder. "You can come out!"

The lip of the balloon rose next to Belle. The girl took a step back, as if getting ready to run, and watched, tense and wary, as Lumiere and Cogsworth emerged. Cogsworth leaned on Lumiere, one arm slung around his shoulder.

"This is Monsieur Lumiere and this is Monsieur Cogsworth," Belle told the girl, indicating the two men. "And I'm Belle. The bird doesn't have a name, but you can name her if you want."

The girl glanced from the men to Belle, assessing them. "Belle, huh? Really? *'Beautiful'?*" She gave Belle a dubious once-over, scowling at the mud and hay covering Belle's arms and legs. "If you say so. I'm Elise, which just means Elise."

"*Enchanté,* Elise." Lumiere began to bow, but Cogsworth cried out in pain and Lumiere quickly straightened up. "Oops. Very sorry, *mon ami.*"

Belle hurried over to grab Cogsworth's other arm. "Can you take us to a doctor, Elise?"

Elise shook her head. "No doctor in Brumeux-ville." She studied Cogsworth for a second and then nodded, coming to a decision. "All right. I'll ask Granny T to fix him, too. She's my *grand-mère*, and she can do *anything*." She jerked her chin, indicating that Belle and the others should follow her.

"What about your sword?" Belle asked.

"Oh, just leave it," Elise said. She glanced over her shoulder at Belle and gave her a sly smile. "It's not really a sword—can't you see that? It's just a branch."

CHAPTER
10

The dirt roads, the straw-roofed shacks, the dark mist . . . it all looked exactly like what Belle had seen in the Magic Mirror. This was definitely the village the Prince had shown her.

Lumiere remembered it, too. "Ah, Brumeux-ville!" he declared. He noticed Elise staring at him suspiciously. "I've been here, you see. . . ."

"If you've been to our village," Elise interjected, "then you should know there's no doctor. Hasn't been one for ages—maybe ever."

"It was several years ago," Lumiere said. "I was a boy, about four or five years older than you. My family and I were traveling—"

"I don't care." The girl marched on, picking up her pace.

Belle and Lumiere struggled to keep up with her. "Can you use your good foot, at least, *mon ami?*" Lumiere begged Cogsworth, who hung between Lumiere and Belle, both legs dragging behind him.

"No," Cogsworth whimpered. "I hurt all over."

"If you do not begin to help support some of your weight," Lumiere warned Cogsworth, "I will collapse right here onto this filthy path, and you will fall with me."

"It's dreadfully low of you, Lumiere, to hit a man when he's down," Cogsworth sniveled.

"You are not down yet, *mon ami*," Lumiere replied. "You are still up, thanks to Belle and me. But not for long." He let out a grunt as they took another step.

Cogsworth sighed and pushed himself up on his uninjured foot. They continued, with Cogsworth alternately limping on his bad foot and smacking the boot of the other into the mud, causing Belle and Lumiere to sway and lurch. It didn't seem to Belle to be much of an improvement over dragging him. Cogsworth weighed just as heavily on her shoulders, and she and Lumiere had to steady themselves again with every other step.

Belle distracted herself from the effort by taking in her surroundings, but the sight failed to cheer her up. The village square was a grim, pale shadow of Villeneuve's lively town center. There was no fountain, just a moss-covered well. A scattering of empty buildings bordered the square. They might have once been shops, but they now

served only as shelter for a few scruffy cats.

The villagers the three friends passed either ignored them or gave them wary, sidelong stares. Elise exchanged nods with a few, but she made no attempt to introduce the visitors. Belle tried offering friendly smiles and periodic *bonjours,* but the villagers just picked up their pace. Occasionally, a little boy or girl would glance at Belle, eyes wide with wonder, but almost immediately, a parent would grab the child's hand and jerk him or her away.

"Don't bother trying to get to know anybody," Elise told Belle. "It's not as if you'll be here long. Right?"

Belle hadn't yet told Elise why she and her friends had come. Before they'd left the hayfield, she had whispered to Cogsworth and Lumiere that they should keep the details of their mission a secret for the time being. When they'd planned the trip, Belle hadn't thought ahead to what they'd

tell any villagers they met, because she hadn't expected to meet any. She'd assumed they'd find the Prince, rescue him, and stay long enough only to right whatever wrong he'd done—or return home immediately and decide how to right the wrong later.

Belle now realized that the rescue she'd imagined had a few missing parts.

Cogsworth let out a whimper. "Are we almost there?"

"It's just around the corner," Elise said. She darted ahead and disappeared around a curving lane. "The house with the red door," she called back.

Belle, Lumiere, and Cogsworth slowly followed. When they finally reached the house, the door was open. Elise, no longer holding the bird, stood in the doorway and impatiently gestured for the group to enter.

The inside of the house was as warm and

colorful as the air was cold and gray. Woven blankets with fanciful designs hung from the clay walls and covered the wooden furniture. A small loom sat in a corner, surrounded by baskets of wool. A modest fire flickered in a stone fireplace.

A slender young woman in a scarf hurried over from the stove. "Please, *monsieur,* have a seat." She helped Belle and Lumiere settle Cogsworth into a rocking chair near the fire.

"These are the strangers from the sky I told you about," Elise said. "That's the 'belle' one." She indicated Belle and then rolled her eyes. "Or so she says."

"*Bonjour,* Belle," the young woman said, taking Belle's hand. "I'm Nicole, Elise's mother."

"*Bonjour,*" Belle replied. "This is Monsieur Lumiere."

"*Enchanté, madame,*" Lumiere said with a deep bow. He realized his ponytail was still loose, and he quickly swept back his hair and retied the ribbon.

"And Monsieur Cogsworth," Belle continued.

"You'll excuse me if I cannot bow as well, *madame*." Cogsworth nodded and gave her a half bow.

"Of course," Nicole replied. "You are all very welcome here." After gesturing for Lumiere and Belle to sit at the small dining table, she returned to the stove and gave a stir to the pot sitting atop it, its contents perfuming the room with a spicy scent. "Carrot and ginger soup," she said. "It'll warm you and your friends after your journey."

A *cheep cheep* sounded behind one of the colorful tapestries, which then magically rose— and Belle realized it wasn't a wall hanging but was attached to the ceiling to act as a room divider. A woman Maurice's age emerged from behind it. She was tall and thin, and her dark hair was flecked with gray. In her hands she held a small round basket.

Cheep!

The bird poked its tiny beak over the top of the basket.

Elise rushed to her grandmother and took the basket. "You did it! You fixed her!"

"I made her a temporary home and bound her wing with some cloth," the woman said. "But time and rest will heal her, not me."

"I told you Granny T can do anything," Elise told Belle proudly.

"My granddaughter exaggerates my skills," the woman said. "I have to admit, though, I rarely discourage her. She'll grow up soon enough."

"Even when I'm a hundred, I'll think exactly the same way about everything as I do now!" Elise protested. She moved to the hearth and sat down, holding the basket on her lap.

"I hope not," the woman said with a smile. She turned to Belle. "I'm Granny T. Elise calls me Granny T because when she was a baby, *grand-mère* was too hard to say. She started calling me

Gran Tine, and that became Granny T." Granny T approached Cogsworth. "And this is the other injured party, I presume."

"At your service, *madame*—or rather, at your mercy," Cogsworth said. Granny T drew up a stool and sat down in front of him. She gently squeezed his ankle, causing Cogsworth to whimper.

"Nothing broken," Granny T concluded. "Just a slight sprain, I believe. Easy to treat. We'll soak it in cold water to reduce the swelling."

A wooden shutter in the wall between the stove and the hearth swung open. A bearded man Nicole's age, who shared Elise's sandy hair and dark eyes, leaned through the opening. He held an armload of chopped logs, which he dropped into an iron bin on the floor. They landed with a loud clatter. Spying Belle and Lumiere, he paused. "Oh. Hello there," he said, before pulling the shutter closed.

"That's Papa," Elise said.

"My son Paul," Granny T said. "He can be a little abrupt. Don't let it bother you." She stood up. "I'll be right back with that water."

She returned a few minutes later with a bucket of cold water. As she stepped inside, a beam of bright sunlight swept in past her. Belle and the others blinked.

"The sunshine's a surprise, I know," Nicole said.

"It usually shines by the end of the day," Granny T explained. "If only for a couple of hours."

"Just as I remember!" Lumiere said.

"He says he's been here before," Elise said.

"You may remember my family," Lumiere said. "*La Famille des Chansons*. We were performers when I was a boy. I sang and played accordion."

Granny T shook her head. "I was probably in Paris then with Paul. Nicole may remember, though. She's lived here all her life and would have been a girl when you visited."

"I've lived here all my life, too!" Elise said.

"So far," Granny T replied with a wink. She lowered Cogsworth's foot into the bucket. He yelped. "Even though it's spring, the water comes down from high in the hills," she told Cogsworth, patting his knee. "That's what makes it so cold." He pressed his lips together and nodded bravely.

Granny T turned to Lumiere. "So is that why you've come here? To see the village where your family performed? I'll warn you, you'll find a lot has changed over the years. Except, of course, the fog."

"Ah, no! We have come to—" Belle reached under the table and poked Lumiere in the ribs. "That is to say, uh . . ." He glanced at Belle, who gave him a warning look. "We, um . . ."

"We're servants," Belle said, blurting out the first thing she could think of.

"*Oui!*" Lumiere exclaimed.

"We are indeed!" Cogsworth agreed, perking up a bit.

"In a mansion in a kingdom up north," Belle continued. "Lumiere oversees the dining hall, Cogsworth runs the household staff, and I . . . I'm the governess. We've come because a friend—one of the other servants—disappeared."

Lumiere, eager to be part of the fabrication, joined in. "He's a stable hand—"

"—valet," Cogsworth said at the same time.

"It's a small household," Belle explained. "Some of the servants do double duty."

"I see," Granny T said.

"Our friend mentioned your village recently, so we thought he might have come here," Belle continued.

"The people you work for didn't mind you all leaving at the same time on such a long journey?" Nicole asked.

Belle was about to answer, when Cogsworth spoke. "There's only the master, and he ordered us to go," he said. "He's a generous and thoughtful

man who cares for all of us. We've been through so much together over the years, you see."

"Mais oui!" cried Lumiere, ignoring Belle's pleading look to stop talking. He lowered his voice to a dramatic baritone, as if emoting from a stage. "The master and our friend the stable hand/valet are very, very close." Belle poked him again, but he was too caught up in his performance to notice. "They are *so* close, in fact, they are practically brothers."

"They are so close, they are practically the same person!" Cogsworth declared. He and Lumiere erupted into giggles.

"They're giddy from all the excitement," Belle said, and was relieved when Granny T and Elise seemed to accept the explanation.

Granny T removed Cogsworth's foot from the cold water and wrapped the ankle tightly with a fresh strip of burlap. Belle and Lumiere then helped Granny T settle Cogsworth on one of the

small mattresses in the room behind the tapestry.

"This is Granny T's and my room," Elise explained as Granny T propped Cogsworth's injured leg up on a small stack of folded blankets.

"It's our guest's room, for the present," Granny T told Elise. "Monsieur Cogsworth needs rest and quiet for the next few hours, and this is the best place in the house for it." She adjusted the pillows behind Cogsworth's head.

"You are much too kind, *madame,*" Cogsworth said.

While Cogsworth was resting, Nicole continued making dinner. It turned out she *did* remember Lumiere's family performing in the village. When he launched into one of the many songs from their act, Nicole joined in.

"We used to sing that around the fire in the square after you left," Nicole said wistfully. "Those were happier times in Brumeuxville." Lumiere offered to help with dinner, and Nicole eagerly

accepted, on the condition that Lumiere sing another song or two for her. Lumiere didn't need to be asked twice.

Because the meal would take some time to prepare, Belle asked Elise to lead her back to the hayfield. Now that the fog had cleared, it seemed like a good time to assess the wreck, before it was too dark out. Belle wanted to see if there was enough of the balloon left for them to repair it easily. She wasn't hopeful, but repairing it was the only way they could return home quickly if the Prince had lost the Magic Atlas.

Granny T offered to come along, and she invited Paul as well. As they walked through the village, Belle gave Paul her made-up explanation for their visit. Elise ran several yards ahead, impatient to explore the crash site.

"I think you've come to the wrong place," Paul told Belle. "There haven't been any strangers here for some time. Not until you three. The roads to

the village are a mess. We used to be able to travel out of the kingdom easily—to trade at markets and bring in new goods—but storms and neglect have cut us off. We keep hoping the king will do something to fix the roads, but that hope's fading fast."

Belle remembered the grimness of the castle they'd flown past. It seemed as if the bleakness of the village was reflected by the residents of the castle. Her heart ached at the thought of the Prince being trapped in such a place. And she was still confused as to how he could be blamed for the kingdom's troubles. How could one person be responsible for such oppressive gloom?

"Why won't the king help?" Belle asked.

"Our queen died a few years ago," Paul said. "After she did, the king locked himself up in his castle. He forgot us."

Belle wanted to ask about the queen she'd seen in the mirror, but then she'd have to explain how she knew about her. Elise might believe a Magic

Mirror could exist, but Belle didn't think Paul would. Granny T she wasn't sure about yet.

"Now and then someone ventures out of the kingdom, through the woods to the river, or over the hills to the sea," Paul said as they caught up with Elise at the edge of the field. The sun was setting between the hills, partially hidden by a gauzy cloud that cast the peaks in a rosy blush. The pink twilight caused the debris strewn around the hay to twinkle like chips of silver. "But it's rare. Rarer still for somebody to come to us."

"Their friend could have flown a machine here!" Elise suggested. "Like they did!"

Paul gazed around at the wreckage in wonder. "A hot-air balloon that eats clouds!" He shook his head and laughed. "I sure would've liked to see it in flight." He picked up a bent pipe and examined it. "It sounds like something out of one of those wild stories my mother tells Elise."

"You used to like those stories when you were

young, Paul," Granny T said. "You had quite the imagination then. Your daughter gets it from you."

"I think it skips a generation," Paul said with a wry smile. "I'm not quite as fanciful as the two of you."

Belle surveyed the hunks of metal and shards of wood. It didn't take her long to realize there was no way they'd be returning to Villeneuve the way they'd come.

"I hope you know you and your friends are welcome to stay the night with us," Paul said, guessing at her thoughts.

"Or as long as it takes for your friend's ankle to heal," added Granny T.

Paul nodded. "We can find a way to get you to the river once you're ready to leave. I'm sure you'll be able to catch one of the barges going north."

"Thank you," Belle said. "And I promise we'll clean up this mess before we leave."

"Look, Granny! A *real* sword!" Elise swung a

piece of the steam-valve rod in the air—*swoosh, swoosh!*

"Careful, Elise!" Paul warned. He turned to Belle. "Your machine may be a loss to you," he said, "but I'm sure I could find other uses for these parts."

"Nicole would love to have this material to make clothes," Granny T said as she examined a long shred from the silk balloon. "Maybe even curtains!"

"Please, take anything you want," Belle said. She'd feel better if what was left of the balloon didn't go to waste, and she knew her father would feel the same. Elise's family had been so generous already. This seemed like the least Belle and her friends could do to pay them back.

While Elise helped Granny T fold the remnants of the silk balloon and Paul gathered the crushed pipes and scraps of cedar, Belle made her way quietly to the edge of the field, where she'd noticed

a charred patch in the hay. When she got close enough, she spotted a familiar orange glow in the dirt. She smiled.

She'd found the Magic Stone.

She considered picking it up, but she couldn't hold it without burning herself, and slipping it into her pocket was likely to set her dress on fire. She could carry it out in one of the metal scraps, but then she'd have to explain to Elise's family what it was.

She decided the best thing to do was to leave it for now. She grabbed a curved fragment of tin lying nearby and dug a hole deep in the ground a few feet away. Using the tin, she rolled the glowing orb toward the hole until it fell in. She covered it with dirt and hay and stood back. There was no glow. If she hadn't just buried it, she wouldn't have been able to distinguish its hiding place from the rest of the uncharred ground around it.

The Magic Stone was safe for now.

CHAPTER 11

Because there wasn't enough room at their small dining table for everyone, Elise's family and their guests gathered on stools around the hearth to eat dinner. Cogsworth had eaten earlier and was once again resting in the blanketed-off room.

Lumiere insisted on serving the meal, which he did with a flourish. After spinning around on one

foot, he swooped down and delivered each bowl of soup without spilling a drop. He then juggled five spoons in the air, catching them and handing them out one at a time to the diners, and did the same with the rolls.

"*Voilà!*" he exclaimed when he had finished. The others applauded.

"*Merci!*" Lumiere said with a bow. "*Bon appétit,* everyone!"

"*Bon appétit!*" they all replied.

Belle saw Elise slip a piece of bread to the bird, which sat in its basket at her feet. Elise caught Belle watching and pressed a finger to her lips.

"I saw your loom," Belle said, drawing the adults' attention to the opposite corner of the room. Elise gave her a grateful smile.

"It's Nicole's," Paul said proudly. "She made all the blankets you see hanging in here."

"The designs are beautiful," Belle said.

"*Très belle,*" agreed Lumiere.

Nicole beamed. "Thank you. I used to sell them at markets in towns along the coast. Now that travel is so difficult, I make them for us, and we occasionally use them to barter with."

"We have a farm plot," Paul said. "But the soil became infested with worms, so now we trade blankets for produce. I also help out on my neighbors' farms, and with shearing the other villagers' sheep in return for more wool, and—"

CHEEP!

The songbird had craned its head toward Elise's hand, hungry for more bread.

"Elise, that bread is for *you* to eat, not the bird," Nicole scolded. "I told you to leave your little friend in your room while we have dinner."

"But Monsieur Cogsworth was snoring! Petra doesn't want to have to listen to *that* while she's trying to get better."

Belle looked at Elise in surprise. "Petra? That's an unusual name."

"Not so unusual!" Elise said. "It's the name of the enchanted princess in—"

"*The Kingdom in the Clouds,*" Belle said.

Elise stared at Belle in shock. "How did you know?"

"It's my favorite book," Belle told her.

"It's *my* favorite book!" Elise declared. She jumped up, ignoring her parents' protests, and dashed behind the blanket wall. She returned clutching a dog-eared book with a tattered cover. Its spine had been broken in so many places, it barely held together. A ragged ribbon was tied around the outside to keep the yellowed pages from falling out.

"I *own* it," Elise said proudly. "Granny T gave it to me. It's the only book in the village!"

"Is that true?" Belle asked the others. She couldn't imagine growing up in a village with only one book.

"Not much use for books here," Paul said.

"Except as insulation." He nodded toward the walls, and Belle now noticed book spines poking from the clay.

"I brought those back with me from Paris," Granny T said sadly. "But the damp weather here caused them all to rot before I could figure out a safe way to store them."

"Because we live in a valley, the fog gets trapped," Nicole explained.

"It's even worse in spring and summer," Paul said. "The warmer temperatures pull in clouds from the sea on the other side of the mountains."

"Granny T's books didn't *all* rot!" Elise said, hugging *The Kingdom in the Clouds*. "She kept this one in a special box."

"I'm so glad she could save it for you," Belle said to Elise. Then she turned to Granny T. "But I'm so sorry about your other books." Belle pictured the thousands of books in the royal library shriveling up and disintegrating before

her eyes, then shook off the horrible image.

Nicole noticed Lumiere washing the dishes. "*Monsieur!* We cannot have a guest clean up!" She rushed over to him.

"Too late, *madame*," Lumiere replied, drying the last dish. "And it was my pleasure."

Paul went outside to collect more wood while Nicole helped Lumiere and Belle stack several blankets around the softly roaring fire for Granny T, Elise, and Belle to sleep on.

Lumiere agreed to sleep on the floor next to Cogsworth. "I shall endure his snoring," Lumiere said bravely as he slipped behind the tapestry wall. He was soon fast asleep and snoring himself.

"Tell us a story!" Elise begged Granny T.

Nicole shook her head. "It's getting late, Elise," she said.

"I'm not tired!" Elise protested.

"We know *you're* not," Granny T told Elise. "But Belle probably is."

"I'd love to hear a story," Belle said. "A true one. About Brumeux."

"Oh, yes! Yes!" Elise cried, thrilled at the suggestion. "I can tell one! Let me tell it." She climbed onto a stool and held up her hands. "Once upon a time," she began, her voice low and serious, "there was an enchanted princess, like Petra." Elise gestured to the songbird, now sleeping peacefully in its warm basket at the end of Elise's blanket bed. "Her name was Marianne, and she lived in an enchanted castle."

"You know Princess Marianne isn't *really* enchanted," Nicole said to Elise.

"Yes she is!" Elise insisted. "You believe me, don't you, Belle?"

Belle pictured the darkened castle they'd flown over—and the crowned woman she'd seen in the Magic Mirror. "Does the princess live with the king?" she asked.

"Yes! Yes! Of course!" Elise said impatiently.

"Her father is King Robert and her mother was Queen Cecile, and that's why she's a princess."

Marianne was Cecile's daughter, which made her the Prince's cousin. Mrs. Potts hadn't mentioned a cousin when she'd told Belle the story of the twin queens, but she might not have known about her. Did the Prince know? Whether he did or not, one thing seemed clear: it was Princess Marianne who had imprisoned the Prince.

But why?

"Someone cast a spell on her that made her dark with sadness and grief," Elise went on. "She has to keep all the castle gates locked, and she and the king can never leave the castle. Nobody can go in, either."

"In real life it wasn't a spell," Nicole told Belle.

"It was because the queen died," Belle said. Nicole and Granny T nodded. "Paul told me earlier that the king locked himself away after her death."

"That's right," Elise agreed. "He's enchanted, too."

Paul returned with the firewood. "Sorry it took me so long. Rain got into the bin, and I had to dig down to find pieces that weren't soaked." He placed several logs on the burning embers. The flames shot up, crackling as they ignited the new wood. The moisture from the wood turned to steam, and delicate puffs of white rose above the flames and then vanished. As with the steam balloon, the transformation from cold to hot was as amazing as anything in a fairy tale.

It struck Belle that magic was all around them, all the time. This was more proof that made-up stories weren't so far from the truth. Belle understood how the death of someone you loved could cast a kind of spell. Enchantment was just a way to describe something very real. But grief alone didn't explain the behavior of the person she had seen in the Magic Mirror. Why would the Prince's

cousin have locked him in a dungeon? Could Elise be right? Was there some other dark enchantment at work?

"Before Queen Cecile died, it was much different," Nicole said. "After she and King Robert were married, it was like the sun had come out in our village. Even the cloudiest days felt bright and cheerful."

Granny T nodded. "Queen Cecile was special," she said. "The king knew a lot about military affairs and about how to rule. But the queen came from a different background. She loved art and music—and literature."

"She'd planned to build a school in the village," Nicole told Belle. "They started it but never got farther than the outer wall."

Paul poked the fire. "Now that wall is just a pigpen," he said.

"If the queen had lived, we'd have books in this village," Granny T said. "Books for reading, not for

doorstops or to patch holes in walls."

"I wonder why the king didn't finish the school, if it was what the queen wanted," Belle said.

"Because he's enchanted!" Elise said, hopping down from the stool. "I just told you that."

"No, Elise," Granny T said. She turned to Belle. "We heard from a few of the servants who worked in the castle that the queen begged the king to finish the school before she died. But he spent too much money bringing in doctors from all over the country to treat her. She'd caught a rare fever of some sort. No one could cure it."

Paul stood and clapped the ashes from his hands. "The queen died, the servants left, and the school was forgotten, like the rest of the village."

"Now the king and the princess have to wait for someone to break the spell," Elise said.

"That's right, Elise." Granny T opened her arms and Elise ran over for a hug. "Good times always follow bad. Eventually." She kissed the top of her

granddaughter's head. "But now it's time for bed."

Nicole nodded, and after she and Paul had tucked Elise into her blanket bed, they said goodnight and disappeared behind their burlap canopy. Elise waited a moment and then drew *The Kingdom in the Clouds* from under her blanket. "Read us a little, Granny."

Granny T shook her head. "Elise . . ."

"Please? Just the part where Marie finds the palace." Elise held out the book.

Granny T sighed and reached out to take it. "I want you to lie down and close your eyes, though."

Elise yanked up her blanket and squeezed her eyes shut. Belle exchanged a smile with Granny T and tried not to laugh.

"All right. Let me just find the right place." Granny T flipped through the tattered pages.

"This is Granny T's story, you know," Elise whispered to Belle. She peered at Belle through one open eye.

Belle lay down and drew up her own blanket. "I remember," she said. "You told me she gave the book to you."

"That's not what I mean. It's *her* story."

"That's enough, Elise," Granny T said. "No more talking or there won't be time for me to read." Elise closed her eyes again.

"Here we are," Granny T said. "*'Marie had been flying so long on her dragon, she'd lost track of how much time had passed. The clouds hugged them, making it difficult to see above or below.'*"

Belle noticed that although Elise's eyes were closed, her lips moved as she recited the words Granny T spoke.

"*'She caught glimpses of gold through the mist, glimmering and glittering, and then disappearing again.'*"

Instead of reading from the book, Granny T had set it on her lap. She, too, was reciting from memory.

"*As they drew closer, Marie saw a castle gate. It rose so high that its top disappeared into the clouds.*'" Granny T kept her eyes on the fire, which crackled and sparked. "*'Behind the gate was the misty outline of a grand palace.'*"

Belle gazed at the ceiling as she listened. She pictured the enchanted palace floating above her, encased in its cottony cloud bank, its shimmering gates slowly swinging open.

After a few more minutes, Elise's lips stopped moving. She curled onto her side, and Belle could hear her breathing fall into an even rhythm. Granny T smiled down at Belle.

"She has it memorized herself," Granny T whispered. "Even after the book falls apart completely—which won't be too long from now, I'm afraid—she won't have lost it. She'll still have it. Here . . ." Granny T tapped her head, and then her heart. "And here."

"I will, too," Belle said.

"That means a lot to me," Granny T said. In the light from the fire, Belle could see Granny T's smile and the sparkle in her eyes.

"Have you always loved books?" Belle asked.

"I've always loved stories—listening to them and reading them. We did have a few books here in the village when I was growing up. My friends and I would pass them around. They helped me learn there was more to life than the limited experiences I'd had in this small town."

Belle was stunned. Here was someone else who had felt just as Belle had when she was growing up in Villeneuve! Granny T had longed for adventure, and she'd found it, just like Belle.

"So you went to Paris!"

Granny T nodded. "My husband, George, and I. He was a baker." She smiled at the memory. "Life in Paris was as exciting as I'd dreamed it would be. I hope we'll go back one day. I'd love for Elise to see it." She gently set the book next to Elise and

lay down. "Now it really is time for sleep," she said. Her face faded in and out of the darkness in the waning light from the dying fire.

"*Bonne nuit,* Belle."

"Good night."

Belle closed her eyes. Thoughts swirled around in her head—events of the day and tasks that lay ahead. Gradually, however, her breathing slowed to match that of her sleeping companions.

She'd almost fallen asleep when an idea occurred to her. It came and went in a flash—something inspired by the book, but what? Belle opened her eyes and tried to latch on to it, but weariness had made her thoughts hazy and jumbled. The idea slipped away, lost among other ideas and memories and stories.

The last of the fire's orange embers winked out, and Belle closed her eyes again, giving up. . . .

Then, at the last moment, the idea came back.

"That's it!" Belle whispered to herself. She needed to think more about it and work out the details. She might not sleep, but she didn't mind. This was worth lying awake for.

She'd figured out a way to rescue the Prince.

CHAPTER 12

"I think... maybe... yes... let me just set it down softly here...."

"*Mon Dieu,* Cogsworth! Stand up, already!" Lumiere rolled his eyes as Cogsworth tentatively tapped the toe of his bad foot on the straw mat next to the bed.

"Don't rush me, Lumiere!" Cogsworth protested.

"Do you want me to reinjure it?"

"There is no weight on it yet!" said Lumiere. "And you have two people to hold you up, and two more making sure you don't fall."

"And I promise we *won't* let you fall," Belle added.

Cogsworth let out an irritated sniff and allowed Belle and Lumiere to lift him off the bed, his arms wrapped around their shoulders. Granny T and Nicole were ready to grab him if he should suddenly stumble.

"Carefully set your foot down," Granny T instructed.

Cogsworth obeyed, a tense grimace on his face. He squeezed his eyes shut in anticipation of pain. "I think it's down. Is it down?" He tipped his head to the side and peered out of one eye.

"*Oui.* You've landed," said Lumiere. "And you are still alive. *Quel miracle.*"

Cogsworth ignored Lumiere's sarcasm. "I must

say, it doesn't hurt too much. A slight twinge, but . . ." He leaned forward a little, gripping hard to Belle and Lumiere. "Definitely improved from yesterday."

Belle smiled. "It looks like you won't be lame for life after all." She was genuinely happy at his recovery.

"It will keep improving," Granny T promised Cogsworth. "A few more days and you should be walking fine without any help."

"We're back!" Paul called as he entered the house with Elise.

Elise darted forward, holding her branch sword from the day before. "I brought it from the field! Monsieur Cogsworth can use it as a cane," she said.

"Very kind of you, young lady." Cogsworth took the branch and tapped it on the floor. "Seems very sturdy. I shall practice walking with it immediately . . . after a brief rest."

He handed the branch back to Elise and

shot a beseeching look at Belle. Belle nodded to Lumiere, and together they lowered Cogsworth onto the bed.

"I have good news," Paul said. "Our friends Antoine and Jacques are heading out to the river this afternoon to fish. They'll clear the way for us to follow, and I've borrowed a mule and cart from Monsieur LeFer, the blacksmith, in return for some of the scrap metal we collected yesterday. I'll drive you to the river and wait with you until a barge or boat comes by to carry you north."

"That's wonderful!" Cogsworth declared. He turned to Belle. "Why didn't you tell me you'd rescued the Prince?" he asked before she could stop him. "Where is he?"

"*Cogsworth,*" Lumiere hissed, his eyes flashing.

"What?" Cogsworth finally noticed that Elise and her family were all staring at him. "Oh, dear . . . What I *meant* was . . ."

"He meant our friend the valet/stable hand, of

course," Lumiere said quickly. "We call him the Prince because . . . because he is a prince of a guy!"

"Yes!" Cogsworth cried. "That is precisely what I meant!" Drops of sweat appeared around his hairline. *"Precisely."*

Belle's stomach dropped as she mentally scrambled for a way to steer the conversation in another direction—any direction. She'd lain awake most of the night formulating her rescue plan, but she hadn't stayed awake the *entire* night. She'd finally drifted off midthought, exhaustion overtaking her. As a result, she'd been the last one in the house to wake up that morning.

By the time she rose from her bed by the hearth, Nicole and Lumiere were already fixing breakfast, Granny T had rewrapped Cogsworth's ankle, and Paul and Elise had left the house on a mission Belle hadn't been aware of—until now. She'd had no time to fill in Lumiere and Cogsworth on her idea, or to come up with the best way to explain the true

purpose of their journey to their new friends.

The staring continued—but not by Elise, who leapt up and down with excitement. "There's a prince? That's almost better than a monster!" She crossed her arms and looked sharply at Belle. "I want to see him," she demanded. Every other pair of eyes in the room now turned to Belle.

Belle decided the simplest explanation was the truth—the *whole* truth. "We weren't sure what to tell you last night," she began. "It's all so complicated. . . . It *is* true that we came here to find our friend. He's not a stable hand or a valet, though. And we aren't servants in a mansion—"

"We're servants in a *castle*!" Cogsworth chimed in. "A very *large* castle—which I run with meticulous precision."

"We are not *all* servants in the castle," Lumiere corrected him. "Belle merely lives there with her father."

"The castle belongs to the Prince," Belle

explained. "His mother was your Queen Cecile's sister. The Prince knew about the struggles in your village, and I'm pretty sure he came here to see if he could fix things. But something went wrong, and we think he's been imprisoned in your castle. That's why we've come: to rescue him."

Paul shook his head. "Like I told you before," he said, "there's been no news of anyone entering the village in months, or trying to get into the castle. Maybe he never arrived here."

"He's here!" Cogsworth declared. "We saw him get thrown in the dungeon!"

"You saw . . . ?" Paul asked. *"How?"*

"We, um, saw him from our balloon," Lumiere said. "Through the dungeon window."

"The dungeon is belowground," Paul argued. "The windows are at ground level."

"We had a very strong telescope," Lumiere said.

"That's true!" Cogsworth said. "We *did*. Unfortunately, it fell from the balloon and we lost it."

"Which is the truth, *exactement,*" Lumiere said.

Belle sighed. "I don't want to lie anymore." She turned to Elise and her family. "We saw him in a Magic Mirror."

"Magic Mirror!" Elise ran to Belle's side and grabbed her arm. "Let me see it! Let me see it!"

"I don't have it with me," Belle said. "I dropped it before we left, and it broke."

"Of course it did," Paul said with a laugh.

"Belle is telling the truth," Lumiere insisted. "The Enchantress gave the Prince the mirror when—"

"Enchantress!" Elise clapped her hands in delight.

"That's a whole other story," Belle told Elise.

"I want to hear it!"

"I'll tell it to you another time." Belle needed Elise's family to believe her, which meant she had to keep the magic to a minimum. "First we have to rescue the Prince—but we can't do it alone."

"Why would his own family imprison him?" Nicole asked.

"I don't know," Belle said. "Something happened in the past, but he wouldn't tell me what. Once we rescue him, we can find out."

Paul was still unconvinced. "How did the Prince get onto the castle grounds when no one's been allowed through the gates for years? How did he get to the kingdom in the first place?" Belle hesitated, unsure how to answer. "Don't tell me," Paul said. "It was magic."

"Ooo! Did *he* fly, too?" Elise asked.

"In a way," Belle said.

Paul shook his head. "I'm sorry, Belle, but this sounds like something . . . like something out of that book." He waved at Elise's copy of *The Kingdom in the Clouds*.

"I know it does," Belle replied. "But I promise, it's the truth. Will you help us?"

"I believe her," Granny T said.

"Of course you believe her, Mama," Paul said. "You've got the wildest imagination here—even counting Elise."

"I believe her, too!" Elise declared.

"Just because you don't the how or why of something doesn't mean it isn't true," Granny T told her son.

"I believe her, too," Nicole chimed in. "Why would Belle lie? She's obviously come here on a mission that's important to her and her friends. Now she's explaining to us what it is."

"And asking for our help," Granny T added. She turned to Belle. "Which we will give, to the best of our ability."

"Three against one, Papa!" Elise said.

Paul let out a defeated laugh. "Not for the first time." He folded his arms and sighed. "Well, let's hear it, then," he said, addressing Belle. "How can we help?"

CHAPTER
13

Belle explained her idea, and she, Cogsworth, Lumiere, and Elise's family figured out the basic plan. Paul then left with Elise to carry out his part, while Granny T joined Nicole at the loom.

Belle sat with Lumiere and Cogsworth at the fire to work out more of the details. "*I* should play the visiting king," Lumiere insisted. "Due

to my theatrical background, of course."

"I need to be the king," Cogsworth argued. "I'll have to ride in the carriage, don't forget." He waved to his burlap-bound ankle.

"Cogsworth's right, Lumiere," Belle said. "It's better if he acts as the king."

"See?" Cogsworth said. "I'm right yet again." He drew himself up straight in his seat. "I *do* look the part, if I say so myself. And my injury will fit perfectly with my disguise. They'll think I have the gout. It's a very royal illness. Many, many kings have it."

"Lumiere," Belle interjected. "Your role is just as important. As the chief courtier traveling with the king, you have to charm the guards."

"Ah! *Mais oui!*" Lumiere cried, delighted. "I understand now. If charm is what you need, *I* am your man. Cogsworth is *absolument* what I would call inadequate in that department." He ignored Cogsworth's glare.

Belle's idea was inspired by a scene from *The Kingdom in the Clouds*. In it, Marie posed as a visiting princess and tricked the castle guards into letting her through the gates. Belle had combined this with a scene from a different book in which an army snuck its soldiers into an enemy's fortress by hiding them in a giant wooden horse sent to the enemy as a "gift."

Together these two plots made up Belle's plan. Lumiere and Cogsworth would approach the castle gates in a carriage. Lumiere would capture the attention of the guards by explaining that "King Cogsworth" had come from their tiny kingdom in the hopes of forging an alliance. Once the guards had opened the gates, Belle, hiding in a secret chamber inside the carriage, would slip out onto the castle grounds.

"The Magic Atlas is in there somewhere, along with the Prince," Belle explained to her friends. "I just have to locate the window to his cell. Once he

tells me where he last saw the atlas, I'll find it, and we'll use it to escape."

"What if they actually admit us into the castle?" Cogsworth asked. "What do we do then?"

Considering that the grief-stricken king and princess had banned all visitors, it was more likely the guards would send them back out and shut the gates behind them. "If you meet King Robert or Princess Marianne, ask them about the kingdom and its history. The more you can keep them talking about themselves, the less they'll ask about you. Then say you'd like to tour the kingdom and visit the village before dark. If the Prince and I have already left the castle, we can meet you outside the gates, and we'll all leave together."

"We're ready for a fitting!" Granny T called from the other side of the room.

In *The Kingdom in the Clouds,* Marie had a cloak made from magic silver threads given to her by a friendly sorcerer she'd met along her journey.

The cloak could transform into whatever type of clothing Marie wanted—including the royal gown of a princess. Belle and her friends didn't have a magic cloak, but they did have the "magic" Nicole could weave on her loom.

"Monsieur Cogsworth first," Nicole said, holding up a shimmering cape. She'd woven together scraps of blue silk taken from the balloon, and Granny T had sewn on a stripe of fluffy furlike cream-colored wool for the trim.

Belle helped Cogsworth stand, and Nicole and Granny T draped the cape around his shoulders. The cape seemed to act as a tonic to his pain, and he gestured for Belle to step back. Holding tight to his makeshift cane, Cogsworth stood regal and proud, without wavering.

Lumiere studied Cogsworth. "Hmph," he mused. "Not bad."

"We thank you for your kind words, humble courtier," Cogsworth said, with a slight bow of his head.

"The robe makes the man, as they say," Granny T observed. "Or in this case, the king."

While Belle and Granny T helped Lumiere with the satin tunic that had been made for him, Nicole opened the shutter over the window next to the hearth. "Do we have the crown yet?" Nicole called.

A moment later, Elise burst in, carrying a ring of tin. Sharp, triangular points had been shaped along its brim, each adorned with a colorful, shimmering "jewel."

"Some are from a broken glass bottle that Papa chipped into smaller bits and polished," Elise said, pointing to each gem. "And some are stones from the river."

Belle placed the crown on Cogsworth's head. He straightened even further, growing taller before their eyes.

"Have you ever seen a magic cloak in real life, Granny T?" Elise asked.

"No, I haven't," Granny T replied. "But that

doesn't mean one doesn't exist somewhere."

"Then how did you know how to describe it in the book?" Elise said.

"Well, I just imagined it. . . ." Granny T caught herself. She exchanged a quick look with Nicole.

"*You* imagined it?" Belle asked, confused. Granny T's cheeks grew pink.

"It doesn't need to be a secret from Belle," Nicole told Granny T. She turned to Belle. "Granny T wrote *The Kingdom in the Clouds.*"

"I told Belle that already, last night," Elise said.

"Yes, but I thought . . ." Belle shook her head. It didn't make sense. "The author's name on the book is—"

"Pierre LeFaux," Granny T answered. "I know."

"That man's only a name on the cover," Elise said. "He stole it from her. Tell her, Granny T."

"To be fair," Granny T said, "he didn't steal it. I gave it to him—foolishly. Pierre LeFaux owned the publishing company. He liked the book but

refused to publish it under my name. 'Women don't write books,' he said." She sighed. "I was a young mother, and George was struggling with his bakery. We needed the money the publisher offered me. I trusted him, so I let him put his own name on it. When the book became popular, he claimed true authorship—and kept the profits."

"Quelle horreur!" Lumiere declared. Cogsworth nodded in agreement.

"George and I tried to fight, but it was impossible," Granny T said. "We didn't have a formal contract, and no one believed it was my book. We ran out of money, and eventually we decided to move back here to the village."

"Did you ever write any other books?" Belle asked.

Granny T shook her head. "Maybe someday..."

Paul leaned his head in the front door. "Is the king ready for his carriage?" he asked.

Paul introduced Belle, Cogsworth, and Lumiere to
Monsieur LeFer, the blacksmith, a large, burly man
with a bushy black beard.

"These lads are my apprentices," Monsieur
LeFer said, indicating two skinny teenage boys
standing behind him. "Sebastian and Bernard."
The boys nodded shyly.

Elise held up her new steam-valve rod sword.
"The royal carriage is this way!" she said. She led
Belle and the others around the side of the house.

"It's actually a donkey cart," Paul explained,
catching up with Belle and Elise. "But thanks to
the parts from your steam balloon, it's—"

"Incroyable!" Lumiere exclaimed.

"Indeed! Incredible!" Cogsworth echoed.

Belle circled the cart-turned-carriage, studying
it in amazement.

Pieces of steel from the balloon's boiler had

been soldered together and attached to the cart, with lumber from the cedar basket used for the carriage doors. The doors had been painted a lustrous royal blue and were adorned with glass beads and river stones. The polished steel sides gleamed, setting off the landscape design chiseled into the metal. There was a canopied seat at the front, where Lumiere would sit.

"Always dreamed of being an artist," Monsieur LeFer said in response to the awed admiration of Belle and the others. "Hammering into steel's as close as I got."

"You *are* an artist," Belle insisted. The others agreed.

The body of the carriage was a strange, angular shape, but its oddness added to its impressiveness. It was something an eccentric king would commission. It would certainly capture the castle guards' attention while she slipped away unnoticed.

Paul opened a panel at the back of the carriage to reveal the space where Belle would hide.

"Ah, here he is!" Monsieur LeFer gestured behind him to a tall, mustached young man leading a sturdy black horse by the reins.

"Antoine has agreed to lend you his horse," Paul explained.

"Coco has made the journey before and knows the roads," said Antoine. "He'll keep you on the right path."

"Thank you," Belle told Antoine. She smiled at the horse and stroked his mane. "And thank *you*, Coco."

The horse whinnied in response.

"It should take you about an hour to get to the castle," Paul said. "It looks like you'll have decent weather."

He pointed to the sky. It was still gray, but there was a glow to it, hinting at the sun hiding behind the clouds.

"Rain can come suddenly here, though," Granny T warned.

"We have experienced that firsthand, *madame*," Cogsworth said.

"What happens if *you* get captured, too?" Elise asked.

Belle shifted her gaze to Lumiere and Cogsworth. They hadn't discussed the possibility, but Belle knew they were aware of it. As she met their eyes, an unspoken agreement passed among them: their plan was worth the risk, because it was the best chance they had.

"We came to rescue the Prince," Belle told Elise. "We can't leave without trying. If we're caught, then . . . we'll still have tried."

"And we will keep trying," Lumiere said.

"Even behind bars," Cogsworth added.

Belle smiled and reached out to take the hands of her two friends.

"It's not so grim as all that," Paul said. "We're

not going to let any of you rot in a dungeon. If necessary, we'll gather every single villager and break down the castle walls."

"We will!" Elise said, raising the steam-valve rod above her head. "Don't forget—I still have a sword!"

CHAPTER 14

Belle fidgeted inside the carriage's hidden compartment, trying to get comfortable. Every bump in the rocky road jolted along her spine. Her legs bent at awkward angles no matter how she adjusted them, so that one leg was always falling asleep. Granny T and Nicole had lined the compartment with several wool blankets, but the

blankets had bunched up around Belle's hips and shoulders as she shifted back and forth. They now served less as padding than as annoying additional passengers, rudely hogging the space.

"...and verily I offer to you, fellow Majesty and Highness..."

Belle took her mind off her cramped, bruised body by listening to the muffled voice of Cogsworth, practicing his attempts at "royal" speech.

"...the regal-est of regal friendships—a 'regal-ship,' if you will—"

"Regal-ship?" Lumiere's voice rose above Cogsworth's. "Do you want them to lock us up before Belle has even started her search?"

"It's a king's prerogative to make up words," Cogsworth replied haughtily.

"Where did you learn that? Did you *make it up?"* Lumiere sighed. "I think it might be better if we pretend you're mute, *mon ami.* I'll do all the

talking, and you can just make hand signals."

Belle laughed to herself as Cogsworth sputtered in protest—until the carriage hit another bump, and her head thumped against the roof of the compartment. "Ow!"

"Belle!" Lumiere hissed. "You're supposed to remain silent. You're lucky we're not near the castle yet."

"I know," Belle called up. "I'm sorry. These bumps—"

"Try to steer better, Lumiere," Cogsworth instructed. "Pay less attention to me and more to the road."

"I am steering *perfectly*. I cannot make the road less bumpy." He paused. "But I *can* slow down the horse, if that will help," he called to Belle.

"No. I'll be fine," she said. "I don't want us to get caught in a storm and—"

Her words were interrupted by a loud *ping*ing against the metal carriage.

"I am afraid it is too late for us to outrun the rain," Lumiere said. Within seconds, the *ping*ing had increased to pounding, which was accompanied by a loud crack of thunder.

"Ach!" Cogsworth shouted. "My royal robe!"

"Mon Dieu!" Lumiere said. "I'm afraid our carriage is not quite watertight."

Belle yelled for Lumiere to stop. "I need to get out for a minute!"

"But, Belle, you'll get wet," Lumiere protested.

"That doesn't matter! It's more important that you two not show up at the castle gates drenched. Rein in Coco and let me out."

Five minutes later, Belle was back inside the compartment, but without the blankets. She'd draped one over Coco and the rest over the roof of the carriage and the driver's-seat canopy.

Belle no longer had any padding to protect her legs and arms from the soldered seams of the wagon poking into her with each bump. Her

clothes were soaked. She hugged herself and tried not to shiver as the journey continued. She closed her eyes and pictured herself back at the castle, seated by a fire with Maurice and the Prince. The fantasy warmed her for a few seconds, and she forgot where she was—until she was thrown against a wall of the compartment as the carriage abruptly stopped.

"We've arrived, Your Majesty!" Lumiere called loudly.

"Wait!" Cogsworth said in an urgent whisper. "I forgot what I'm supposed to say. Give me a minute." Belle clenched her fists, willing Cogsworth not to panic.

"Don't worry, *mon ami*," Lumiere said, his voice calm and soothing. "*I* am the one to speak first anyway. You're a king. You speak only to royalty. I will deal with the guards."

Belle shifted to face a trapdoor that would let her sneak out of the compartment.

"Hmm. I don't see any guards, however," Lumiere continued. "I wonder if—"

"WHO GOES THERE?" a voice boomed from somewhere above them. Belle guessed the guards were stationed in a tower on a wall at the top of the castle. "NO ADMITTANCE!"

"Bonjour!" Lumiere called brightly, as if the guard had merely uttered a friendly hello. "I am Monsieur Lumiere, chief courtier of King Cogsworth, His Royal Majesty of La Petite Ville à Côté de la Mer. We have come to—"

"NO ADMITTANCE!" the guard yelled louder.

"Ah, but we are here to see King Robert and Princess Marianne."

"His Majesty and Her Highness are not accepting visitors."

"Princess Marianne is expecting us."

"Expecting . . ." There was a pause, and Belle could just make out two arguing voices, still coming from high above. "La Petite Ville

de *what*?" the guard called down.

Lumiere coughed. "*Pardon, messieurs.* My throat is a little—*eh, eh*—scratchy. We had not prepared for the . . . shall we say, your 'temperamental' weather here." His voice grew quieter and quieter as he spoke. "I'm afraid I may have caught a—*eh, eh*—cold, which makes it difficult to yell. It would be so much easier if you would—"

"What? What? Speak up!"

"I am dreadfully sorry, *messieurs,* but . . ." Lumiere was nearly whispering now. He coughed again, then waited, silent.

A few moments later, Belle heard a loud creak as the gates swung open. She smiled. Lumiere was playing his role perfectly.

"Bonjour encore!" Lumiere said, returning to his normal voice. "It is so nice to meet face to face in this time of gates and walls and impersonal postal correspondence, is it not?" He shook Coco's reins and the horse *clip-clop*ped forward. "In La

145

Petite Ville à Côté de la Mer, it is sunny every day! You should visit—"

"Hold on a minute!" the guard barked. "You can't come through here."

"We needed to get out of that puddle," Lumiere replied. "The wheels of King Cogsworth's royal carriage were sinking."

"Halt, halt, *halt!*" a second, squeaky voice shouted.

"*Mais oui!* As you see we are only inside enough . . ." Lumiere paused and lightly stomped one foot on the floor of the carriage—a signal to Belle that they were inside the gates. She blew some warm air on her cold fingers and grabbed the handle of the trapdoor. She heard Lumiere leap to the ground. "We shall venture no farther until you two gentlemen say the word," he continued. "Now allow me to explain to you our mission. . . ." His voice grew fainter as he led the guards away from the carriage.

Belle carefully swung open the trapdoor. A gust of cold air blew in on her, sending a chill through her wet clothes. She shivered and felt a sneeze building. She held it in until the urge passed and then quietly climbed out and crept along the side of the carriage, keeping her head low. When she reached the carriage door, she caught Cogsworth's eye through the window. She could sense his nervousness, but he did his best to look confident as he met her gaze. He nodded to her that it was safe to move forward.

Belle continued toward the front of the carriage. The entrance to the castle lay ahead, at the center of an arched stone path bordered by the castle's protective outer wall. She peered around Coco and caught a glimpse of the guards. They were leaning toward Lumiere, who had lowered his voice again, capturing their attention. Belle darted toward the stone path, in the opposite direction from where the men stood.

"Her Highness would have alerted us if she was expecting anybody," Belle heard the squeaky-voiced guard inform Lumiere as she slipped around the side of the castle.

"That is not what Princess Marianne's messenger told *us, monsieur*," Lumiere replied.

"Messenger?" The guard's voice faded as Belle moved farther away. "We would know if she had sent a messenger."

Rainwater pooled in muddy puddles along the path, and the stones were covered with patches of moss. Vines covered the castle walls. Belle glanced up. Just as the base of the castle had disappeared into the mist when they'd flown over it in the steam balloon, the top of the castle was invisible, its towers vanishing into a gray haze.

There was fog in front of Belle, too, as if the moisture in the air had become trapped between the castle and its outer wall. Because the path curved around the castle, she couldn't see the

end of it. It seemed to go on forever.

She searched the base of the ivy-covered castle walls, looking for the barred windows of a dungeon cell, but the vines were thickest at the base of the wall, hiding whatever lay behind them. Belle grabbed a handful and pulled. Thorns pricked her palms as she tore the plant away from the stones.

No window.

She made her way around the castle and continued to tear at the lower vines. Soon her fingers and palms were scraped and bleeding. Mud soaked into her shoes.

"Where are you?" Belle whispered. She thought of how many times she'd asked this question of the Magic Mirror. A sense of hopelessness came over her—why had she thought this rescue would work?

She tore and tore, taking her frustration out on the vines. "There has to be a window. There *has* to." A thick vine resisted her tugging, and she grabbed it in both hands. "Where...are...you?" she asked as

she yanked, her anger building. *"Where . . . are . . ."* The vine came free—and Belle fell backward, slamming down onto the wet stones.

"Belle?" a voice called.

Belle froze. Had she imagined it? There seemed to be only an eerie silence surrounding her.

Then the call came again: "Belle?"

It was a familiar voice. . . .

The voice she had been searching for.

CHAPTER 15

Belle darted toward the sound of the Prince's voice.

"Where are you?" she called in a loud whisper.

"How did you get here?" the Prince replied. Belle followed his voice to a thick patch of vines farther along the wall. "You need to leave," he continued, louder. "*Now*. It's too dangerous for—"

"*Shhh!* The guards will hear you. Lumiere and Cogsworth are still at the gate."

Belle was now on the opposite side of the grounds from where she'd entered, and she could hear Lumiere as she neared the Prince's cell window. *"S'il vous plaît,"* he was saying, "why not just ask Princess Marianne?" Belle had told her friends to leave if they were turned away, but they'd obviously ignored her instructions.

She found the window and pulled away the vines. The Prince's face was barely visible in the darkness of the cell, but a wave of relief came over her—she'd found him.

"You shouldn't have come," the Prince whispered.

"It's too late for that. We're here." Belle extended her arm through the narrow space between two bars. The Prince reached up to take her hand in both of his and squeezed.

"It's so good to see you. . . ." He let go. "But you

have to leave, Belle. *Please.* If anything happened to you . . ."

A sudden sharp wind blew down from above and cut through Belle's wet clothes. She shivered and hugged herself. "We came here to rescue you," she told the Prince. "I'm not leaving unless you're with me." She waited for a reply, but none came. "If you want us—*all* of us—to get home safely, then you'll have to help."

The Prince met her eyes. "How can I help, Belle? I'm locked in a dungeon."

"Where's the Magic Atlas?"

"I don't know."

"I know you used it to get here. It has to be on the grounds somewhere. Did you drop it?"

"No, I . . . It's complicated." The Prince looked away. "There's so much you don't know."

"I know that the woman who locked you up is Princess Marianne," Belle said. "I know she's your cousin."

The Prince's expression was a mixture of admiration and bewilderment.

"I'll explain everything later, after I get you out."

"There's no way to get me out, Belle," the Prince insisted. "Princess Marianne has the atlas. She took my knapsack before locking me up. The atlas was inside."

"Why did she lock you up? Does she know who you are?"

"Yes, that's why she . . . Belle, she's not herself after everything that's happened. I betrayed her. I betrayed her parents."

"How?" Belle asked. "I know Queen Cecile died, and that King Robert and Princess Marianne are devastated, but you aren't responsible for that."

"They asked for my help," the Prince said. "They sent a messenger. I turned him away without even finding out who had sent him. I turned everyone away back then. King Robert had sent him to ask

me for money so they could finish the school here. I didn't know Queen Cecile was dying. I didn't know any of it until later, after the Enchantress cast her spell on me. By then it was too late."

The Prince hung his head, dissolving again into the shadows of the cell.

"You would have helped if you'd known," Belle said, certain this was true. "That's why you came, isn't it? To offer your help now."

"It was no use. Princess Marianne refused to forgive me. I don't blame her."

"You can't give up," Belle insisted. "You can still make it up to them. But we have to get you out of here first."

A gust of wind shook the vines above Belle, knocking free the raindrops clinging to the leaves. They fell on Belle's head, and she brushed them off. "The Magic Atlas is in the castle somewhere. I just need to find it."

"No, Belle." The Prince reached up and grabbed

a bar in each hand, his gaze filled with worry. "You'll get caught."

A raindrop hit the tip of Belle's nose, tickling her skin. She reached up to wipe it off. "I'll figure out a . . . a . . ." A shiver shook her whole body, and she couldn't hold it back: "Ah-*choo!*"

"Who's that!" the squeaky-voiced guard called.

"It came from that way," the other answered.

"It was just a bird," Belle heard Lumiere say. "So musical, no?" But his attempt to fool the guards was drowned out by their shouting. Belle didn't stop to think. She dashed around the way she'd come, the guards' footsteps echoing behind her.

Lumiere stared at her wide-eyed as she neared the front of the castle and the open gates. "Belle . . ."

"Go! Go!" she urged, not slowing, trying to keep her voice down. "Before they—"

"Stop her!" one of the guards shouted.

Belle rushed toward the castle door opposite the gates. "Hurry!" she urged Lumiere over her

shoulder as she threw her body against the door, forcing it open. She entered the castle, stumbling into a large, empty foyer. Gray stone walls rose on either side of her. "She's gone inside!" she heard the squeaky-voiced guard shriek.

Belle raced to the end of the foyer and pivoted to enter a long hallway, hoping Lumiere and Cogsworth had taken the chance to flee. The hallway was nearly as gloomy as the foyer. There were no windows, so the only light came from thick candles set in widely spaced sconces. The footsteps of the guards thundered after her.

A tall, reed-thin butler suddenly stepped into the hallway in front of her, staring at her with a mixture of confusion and alarm.

"Stop her!" the guards shouted again.

Belle darted into a room. There was more light here, but it was filtered through a haze of dust. Dust covered not only the floor, but the furnishings as well. Cobwebs hung from the ceiling corners.

It was as if she'd stumbled into a ruin.

The guards grew closer, and Belle passed through the doorway to the next room. She looked for a place to hide, but this room was as spare and lifeless as the first, with only a few pieces of furniture covered in dust. There were no cabinets to slip into, no curtains to hide behind.

Another passageway led to a rectangular room lined with bookshelves. It looked like a smaller version of the royal library in the Prince's castle—except that the shelves were empty.

Where were the books? Where were the castle's residents, for that matter? Belle didn't have the time to ponder either question—the guards were right behind her. She raced to the doorway at the opposite end of the room and dashed through, only to find herself back in the hall.

A staircase lay ahead, with wide steps leading to the upper levels of the east and west wings. Next to it was a narrower staircase leading down.

Belle took it. After descending about ten steps, she stopped. The guards approached, their boots stomping across the stone floor of the hallway. The stomps grew closer, then paused.

"I don't see her anywhere," Belle heard one of the guards say.

"She must have gone upstairs," the other said.

The steps resumed—*clomp, clomp, clomp*—and then faded away.

She was safe for the moment. She continued carefully down the steps to a lower corridor, which was even darker than the halls upstairs. There were no lamps here, but the hallway was narrow enough that if she stretched her arms wide, she could touch the walls on either side. She used her hands to feel her way, searching for a gap to indicate a doorway.

Her path took odd and sudden turns as she went on. The floor sloped down, and the air around her grew chillier. It felt like she was burrowing

into the earth. She took another step, and her right hand dropped away. She waved the hand around. It touched nothing but air. An opening!

She turned and found the two sides of the open doorway. It took her a second to realize that she could see—sort of. Faint light leaked in through the tiny squares of a vine-covered grate set in the top of the wall opposite her.

She squinted into the dimness. This was definitely not a dungeon cell. It was a vast storeroom of some kind, filled with huge, lumpy forms draped with sheets, like a collection of cloaked, hunched giants. One of the lumps sat in the center of the room, and the rest squatted against the walls.

"She's not down here, I tell you!" a guard's voice echoed down the corridor behind her. Belle rushed to one of the covered forms at the side of the room and grabbed the sheet to pull it up, but it was stuck on something.

"We're wasting time," the guard continued.

"There's no sign of her here. She's gone back outside."

Belle tugged harder, but the sheet still wouldn't move. She squinted into the gloom and discovered that the edges of the sheet were weighted with large paving stones. She pushed one aside, trying not to grunt as the two guards' footsteps drew nearer, then raised the sheet.

She paused at what she saw: stacks and stacks of books, carelessly thrown on top of each other in erratic piles. She sniffed, the rank scent of mildew wafting up from the volumes closest to the floor.

"I can't see anything," the squeaky-voiced guard complained. Belle billowed the sheet up, ducked under it, and drew it around her. "We need to go back and get a torch."

"You should have brought one with you," said the other guard. The chill of the room sank into Belle's still-damp clothes. As if she hadn't already been cold enough, the icy stone floor against

the soles of her shoes made her even colder. She hugged herself as she fought hard to hold back another shiver.

"Me?" the guard said. "Why me? Why not—"

"What is going on here?"

This was a new voice—a female voice—coming from farther down the hall.

"Your Highness, we—"

"What are you doing down here in the dark? You know the storeroom is off-limits."

It was Princess Marianne.

"We're looking for the girl—"

"Girl? What girl?" the princess demanded.

"She snuck through the gates after that fake king and his courtier arrived," the low-voiced guard said.

"You let yet *another* interloper into our castle?" the princess cried in fury. "And no one told me? You dolts!"

"She might have snuck back out while we were

searching," the squeaky-voiced guard said quickly.

Belle silently wished the princess would think the same thing and that they would all go back upstairs. She hugged herself harder as nervousness combined with the cold, causing her to tremble.

"Or she could be wandering around the castle," the princess answered. "She could burst in on my father! Do you want to be responsible for some peasant thief upsetting the king?"

"No, Your Highness," the lower-voiced guard murmured. "We'll—"

"Ah-*choo!*"

Belle winced. The sneeze had burst out before she'd had time to try to stop it.

"What was that?" the princess said.

"It's the intruder!" one guard exclaimed.

"It came from the storeroom," the other said.

Seconds later, Belle heard the men enter the room, followed by the lighter footsteps of the

princess. A thin ribbon of light appeared at Belle's feet as the princess's torch illuminated the space. Belle held her breath, but she knew it was too late. She was as good as caught.

She tried to come up with something to say as she heard the scrape of the paving stones being hauled and the *whoosh* of the sheets being whisked off the lumpy forms one by one. She needed something that would convince the princess she wasn't a thief—without revealing that she knew the Prince.

Between exhaustion and the cold, Belle's mind remained a blank. She barely felt it when the sheet was pulled off her. She barely heard the guards cry, "We found her!"

What she did notice was the sudden blinding light of the fiery torch, and the frightening shadows cast by the monstrous contraption at the center of the room—a tilting wooden structure that looked like it was part rack, part guillotine. Its sheet lay on the ground below it in a twisted heap.

The torch swung toward Belle, and she squinted against its brightness. At first, she saw only the outline of Princess Marianne's face, but then she caught a glimpse of the princess's haunted eyes as they reflected the torch's flickering flames.

The princess wasn't looking at Belle. She was staring at the hundreds of books lining the walls, no longer hidden beneath their sheets. Her eyes were filled with a deep sorrow that Belle had not seen in anyone since she had first met the Beast.

CHAPTER
16

"Why *are* you here?" the princess demanded. "You and your friends? What was your plan?"

"Friends?" Belle asked.

"Don't play innocent with me," the princess said sharply. "It was a bit too much of a coincidence that you slipped in right when your two fellow fools were at the gate. They've been locked

up. They refused to drop their charade—as if I'd believe that story. That silly man with the pocket watch and the tin crown is no more a king than I am a lizard."

Lumiere and Cogsworth had been caught. Belle's heart sank at the news. But at least they hadn't told Princess Marianne their true identities or revealed their connection to the Prince.

"Are you thieves?" the princess continued. "Because if you are, you're the stupidest thieves ever to walk on French soil. What is there here to steal? The kingdom is bankrupt. We had riches once, but they're long gone."

The princess spoke this last sentence to herself, almost under her breath, but Belle could hear the bitterness in it.

"I can see you're determined to remain as mum as your accomplices." The princess turned to the guards. "Take her to the dungeon."

"Wait—" Belle held up her arms as the guards

marched toward her. "There *are* things of value here." She swept her arms out toward the books lining the walls.

"Is *that* what you were after when you broke in here? *Books?*" the princess said. She let out a cheerless laugh as the guards grabbed Belle's arms. "I should have just let you steal them. They're of no use to me. They belonged to my mother."

"But you've kept them." Belle struggled to pull her arms free. "Although you shouldn't store them in this damp room. They're rotting, and—"

"Enough!" The princess gestured to the guards, who dragged Belle toward the door.

Belle twisted free and dashed behind the machine in the middle of the room. "What about *this*?"

"The printing press? A stupid contraption with no purpose."

So it *was* a printing press. Belle had seen pictures of one in books, but she'd never seen one

in person. The guards again charged toward her, but she darted out of their reach. "It *does* have a purpose," she said urgently as the guards lunged for her. "It can save your kingdom."

The princess held up her hand, ordering the guards to stop. "What do you mean?" she asked Belle. "How can this rusty old thing save us?" She shooed the guards into the hall. They hovered there, listening.

"You can clean off the rust." Belle examined the press. It was made up of a long rectangular table, with an upright wooden frame that rose perpendicular to its surface. A huge steel screw stood in the middle of the frame, with a handle attached to its thick base.

"That's not the point," the princess said. "My mother bought this thing to print books for the village school she was going to build. We could afford the labor and supplies then. But she died, and her dream died with her. In a way, my father

did, too. And then the whole kingdom died."

Belle caught another glimpse of the sadness she'd seen earlier in the princess's eyes.

"We never even finished building the school," the princess went on bitterly. "Much less printed any books for it."

"You *have* the supplies, though," Belle said. She'd noticed that not all the uncovered stacks were books. One was a wide roll of paper. Another was a group of several large canisters filled with a black liquid: ink.

"You're not listening to me," the princess said. "We have no money."

"You can make money."

The princess stared at Belle in shock. "I should have expected a criminal idea from a criminal!" She raised her hand to summon the guards.

"You can make money printing *books*," Belle said quickly. "The few presses in France can't print enough to keep up with demand. There are many

villages that would pay you to print books for them. You'll have enough money to finish building the school, to fix the roads . . . to do whatever else the kingdom needs."

Princess Marianne stared at Belle a moment, pensive. Belle could tell the princess was thinking over her suggestion. "How fast could this thing print books?" she asked.

"Not very fast," Belle admitted. "But if it was automated, it could print a lot."

"Automated? You mean run on its own?" The princess laughed. "How do you expect it to do that? With magic?"

"No," Belle said with a smile. "With steam."

CHAPTER 17

"It should be a lot easier than the steam balloon," Belle told the princess.

They were now in the library Belle had dashed through earlier when the guards were chasing her. The princess had brought in a tablet for Belle to write on, and the two sat together at a desk in the center of the room.

"The library is the one room my father will

172

never enter," the princess had told Belle. "Even with the books gone, it reminds him too much of my mother." She explained that her father had given up on even *trying* to rule after the queen had died. "He seems to have forgotten about the village," she had said, echoing Paul's earlier words to Belle. "I don't officially have any power to do anything, not that I thought there was anything we *could* do, since our wealth was gone."

The princess had seen the steam balloon when it had flown past the castle, and Belle explained to her how the concept could be adapted for the printing press. "You don't have to worry about finding water sources, considering how much rain you get here," Belle said now as she sketched. "You'll need a pump, though, and pipes for the steam to pass through—and valves to control the flow of the steam." She showed the princess her finished drawing.

"Where am I supposed to get all *that*?"

"In the village." Belle described how she and a

few other villagers had gathered the parts from the steam balloon after it had crashed. "I doubt they've found other uses for all of the parts yet, and I'm sure they'll be happy to give them to us once they know it will help finish the school and restore the kingdom."

Princess Marianne stood, sketch in hand. "If you can make this press work, I'll let you go, along with that imitation king and fake courtier."

"I can't build it by myself, though," Belle said.

"Fine. Your friends can help. I have enough guards to keep an eye on all three of you."

"I need my father. Papa is the inventor. He built the steam balloon. *I* can help *him*, but without him, I'm only guessing." Belle didn't dare suggest enlisting the help of the Prince—not yet. She knew she'd have to tell the princess the truth eventually, but she wanted to wait until Marianne had developed enough faith in the book printing idea. Once the princess felt certain of a renewed future for

the kingdom, she might be ready to let go of the resentments of the past. "Plus," Belle added, "he has the tools we'll need."

Princess Marianne sighed. "Fine, fine, fine." She waved at the tablet. "Go ahead and write a note to your father explaining everything. After the guards get back from the village with the parts, I'll send them to collect your father and bring him back here tonight."

"Villeneuve is too far for them to return that fast, but while we're waiting, we can at least clean off the press and ..." Belle noticed that the princess was staring at her and felt a sinking in her stomach as she realized what she'd done.

"Villeneuve?" Princess Marianne sprang from her chair, her expression hardening into rage. "What. A. *Coincidence.*"

"Wait, I—"

"Guards!" Princess Marianne shrieked.

"I can explain!"

"Oh! I'm sure you can!" Princess Marianne's chilly smile was laced with fury. "I'm sure there's a perfectly *fantastic* explanation for why you and the Prince just happen to come from the same place. I have one, too: you *know* him."

The guards entered and seized Belle as Princess Marianne tore Belle's sketch to bits. "I should have known when you showed up only days after he arrived. I'm such a fool! He's the reason you're here. *He's* the thing you wanted to steal."

As the guards dragged her downstairs, Belle tried to convince Princess Marianne that the printing press idea wasn't a trick, but the princess refused to believe her. "To think I would have let you and your accomplices loose in the castle!" the princess declared. "And even brought another one of your partners in crime here! Your supposed 'Papa'! As if I weren't fool enough already, I would have willingly armed you with 'pipes' and 'cranks' and 'valves'!"

Belle denied all of it, but the princess wouldn't listen. When they reached the dungeon, Princess Marianne ordered the guards to put Lumiere in with Cogsworth and had them toss Belle into the now-empty cell. The Prince watched from the far end of the dungeon, his hands gripping his cell's bars as he begged the princess to let Belle and the servants go. "They only came to help me," he pleaded. "There's no reason to punish them."

"Don't worry, cousin. I can't afford to feed all four of you forever. Your 'friends' will spend the night here and then the guards will transport them out of the kingdom at dawn." The princess glared at Belle. "You'll be dropped off halfway between here and Villeneuve, and you can find your way home from there on foot. If you have any notions about coming back, know that the guards will be on alert. I may not be so lenient next time." The guards slammed Belle's cell door shut.

"At least let them have the book of maps I brought in my satchel, to help them find their way," the Prince called from his cell.

Princess Marianne peered suspiciously toward the Prince. "They found their way here fine, didn't they?"

"Yes, but we were in our balloon," Belle said, jumping in. "We were able to see the route clearly from above."

"Ah, *oui*," Lumiere added. "Without a map, we might wander for days, into forests—even jungles!"

"There are no jungles in France," Princess Marianne scoffed. "And why should I care how long it takes you?"

"We may starve!" Cogsworth cried, sounding genuinely frightened. "Or worse! Your Highness, if you have an ounce of compassion—"

"*Compassion!*" Princess Marianne marched down the row of cells and back, glaring at the captives. "How dare any of you speak to me of

compassion! What compassion have you—" She reached Belle's cell again and met Belle's pleading gaze. Belle could see the hurt in the princess's eyes at what she viewed as a betrayal of her trust.

"I'm so sorry," Belle told her softly. "I did lie to you about knowing the Prince. But I didn't lie to you about wanting to help."

A flicker of doubt passed over Princess Marianne's face. For a moment, Belle hoped the princess might change her mind and let them continue their plans for the press.

Instead, the princess turned away and reached into the shadows near the dungeon entrance. When she straightened up, she had a knapsack in her hands. She removed the atlas and paged through it. Satisfied that it didn't contain any hidden weapons, she tossed the book through the bars to the floor of Belle's cell. "Fine. Take it. The last thing I need here is another book." She spun around and marched out.

Belle picked the book up off the floor. The embossed gold title glittered up at her in the flickering light from the dungeon wall sconces: *The Geography of the World*.

"You need to get the atlas down to me," the Prince said. "It only works on my command. Then I can get you all out of here."

"Yes. *All* of us," Belle said. She dropped the book outside the bars of her cell and gave it a push. It slid along the floor to Lumiere and Cogsworth's cell next to her, and Lumiere then shoved it on. The Prince reached through the bars and grabbed it.

A moment later, the Prince appeared outside Belle's cell, holding up the cell's keys.

"Soon we'll all be back in Villeneuve," he said.

Belle pushed his hand away from the lock. "No," she said. "You have to go alone." She told him about her plan for the printing press. "The guards might return before dawn, but we'll be able to stall them as long as they think we're all still here."

Belle instructed the Prince to unlock the cell next to her so that Cogsworth could move into the Prince's former cell. After the Prince relocked the cells, Cogsworth crouched down, hidden by his cape to resemble the Prince. Lumiere fashioned a burlap-covered lump in his cell to represent Cogsworth. "If the guards come, we'll pretend to be sick," she explained. "To have all caught chills from the damp weather. We'll tell the guards to ask the princess if we can stay one more day—you'll be back with Papa long before that."

"It seems risky," the Prince said, returning to Belle's cell. "You've already endangered yourself enough."

Belle reached through the bars and laid her hand on his arm. "My mind is made up, and you know what that means."

The Prince sighed and allowed a reluctant smile. "Unfortunately, yes."

"Then stop wasting time! Go!"

CHAPTER 18

Belle paced her cell as she waited for the Prince to return.

"They should be here by now," she whispered to Lumiere and Cogsworth, who were still crouched in their cells nearby.

Just then, Belle heard footsteps.

"Belle!" came her father's voice as he appeared

in the dungeon corridor, the Prince right behind him. "Are you okay?"

"I am now," replied Belle. The Prince used the Magic Atlas to free Belle, then Lumiere and Cogsworth. Belle embraced her father, being careful of his injured arm.

"The Prince told me your plan," said Maurice, "and I think it could work. I'll help you however I can."

Together, the five snuck down the corridor and surprised the guards. Before they knew what was happening, the Prince had used the Magic Atlas to transport them far away from the kingdom. It would take the guards at least a day to get back to Brumeux, if not longer.

Belle led the others through the basement hallway to the storeroom. Using the light of a single candle they'd brought from the dungeon, she showed them the printing press.

"It should be much easier to get working than

the balloon," said Maurice, examining the device. "*If* you can collect those parts."

That was the next step. Using the atlas again, Belle and the Prince arrived at Elise's home, landing in front of the hearth just as the family was sitting down to supper.

"How . . . ?" Paul began, then swallowed, as if the rest of his question had gotten caught in his throat.

"Magic!" Elise declared, bursting from her chair. She turned her excited gaze toward the Prince. "And *you're* the Prince!"

"I am," the Prince confirmed. He bent down to shake Elise's hand. He then did the same with the rest of the family members.

"We don't have time now to tell you everything that happened at the castle," Belle said. "We *can* tell you why we're here, though." She explained her idea for the printing press. "We need the parts from the steam balloon to make it work."

Paul hurried out to collect the remaining scraps of tin and wood from the other villagers, and within the hour, Belle and the Prince had everything they needed to transform the press into a steam-powered machine.

Almost everything, that is. They still needed a safe power source to test the press.

Before returning to the castle, Belle led the Prince to the field where the balloon had crashed. Even with the silvery light of the moon shining between the two mountain peaks, Belle had a hard time finding where she'd hidden the Magic Stone. She looked for the spot where the stone had burned the grass, but it seemed to have disappeared. The constant rain, combined with the stone's magical heat, must have caused new grass to grow quickly—very quickly.

Belle pulled off her shoes. "What are you doing, Belle?" the Prince asked. "There are still shards of metal around! What if you step on a sharp—"

"I found it!" Belle reached down and tapped her palm on the ground where her foot had felt warmth. The young grass under her hand buzzed with the heat coming up through the dirt. She and the Prince dug until they reached the smooth top of the metal box in which Belle had placed the stone.

Belle smiled. *"Now* we can go back."

"Papa!" Belle shushed Maurice. "Not so loud!"

Maurice paused, hammer in hand, and glanced at his daughter. "A person can hammer only so softly, Belle. I'm being as quiet as I can."

Belle peered out into the hallway. There was nothing but darkness and silence. "I guess if we haven't woken anyone up yet, we aren't likely to." She returned to the press and continued scraping the rust from the central screw. They'd been work-

ing for a few hours now, and she'd already cleaned off the metal plates she'd found under another sheet in one corner of the room. She discovered that each of the plates had already been filled from end to end with individual letters of removable metal type—evidence that Queen Cecile had been preparing to print her first book before she fell ill.

"The walls are thick enough here to hide any sound," the Prince assured Belle.

"And we are far, far below where they are all sleeping," said Lumiere, who had been put to work laying out the damp blank paper to be dried.

"Except for our two guards, of course," added Cogsworth as he struggled to hold up the boiler tank the Prince and Maurice were attaching to the back of the press.

Lumiere snickered. "*Oui!* They are wide awake! No doubt trying to steer clear of bears and wolves as they search for a way out of the forest."

"I left them on a road," the Prince said

defensively. "It was a desolate road in the middle of nowhere," he added with a shrug. "But at least it was a path that should eventually lead them . . . somewhere."

The Magic Stone now sat atop its box along one wall of the storage room. Although it was a safe distance from the books and paper, it sent out more than enough heat to warm the room and dry the paper Lumiere had unrolled. The stone also sent out an orangey glow that blended with the faint golden rays of the lanterns Paul had lent them, which Belle and the Prince had placed around the floor. Light glinted off the corners of the press, the sides of the ink bottles, and the edges of the metal plates, casting diamonds on the walls and making the space seem magical.

Belle finished removing the rust from the screw, then joined her father and the Prince beside the body of the press. "How close are we?"

"Close, I hope." Cogsworth huffed, straining to

keep the boiler aloft. "I can't ... hold this ... much longer." Belle rushed over to help him.

"I just need to attach the crosshead rod to the crosshead," Maurice said. "And the piston rod to the piston . . . and maybe make one or two more tweaks after that."

Belle had occasionally glanced toward the grated window throughout the night, searching for signs of a lightening sky—a warning that dawn was near. She wasn't sure, but it looked like the black squares between the grate's bars had shifted to a dark gray. "We need to hurry. It's almost dawn, and—"

"*Wrong.*"

The voice came from the doorway. Belle and the others looked over to find Princess Marianne glaring at them.

Cogsworth dropped his end of the boiler. It crashed to the stone floor with a deafening *clang*.

"How did you get out?" the princess demanded

as she entered the room. The glow from the lanterns and the Magic Stone caused her shadow to loom dangerously behind her. "What did you do with the guards?" She didn't wait for answers. "What are you *doing* in here? Why is the paper all over the floor? Where did this junk come from? What is that glowing thing? And *who* are *you*?"

This last question was directed at Maurice, and at last the princess paused long enough for Belle to reply.

"This is my father." Belle took Maurice's hand. "I told you about him. He built the steam balloon."

"Not by myself!" Maurice said. He cast proud smiles at Belle and the Prince. "I had a lot of help."

"How lovely that you're such a nice happy family!" the princess exclaimed with false brightness. "Well, then you and your father will enjoy sharing a cell after I have you all locked up again." The princess marched back toward the doorway,

but before she could call for more guards, Belle dashed in front of her, blocking.

"You asked what we were doing here," Belle said. "But you already know the answer."

The princess shrugged. "It's too late for you to win your freedom by pretending to fancy up the printing press," she said. "The deal was off once I knew you and the Prince—"

"We're not doing it for *us*," Belle interrupted. "We escaped from our cells. The atlas the Prince brought with him is magic. That's how he got here and how we got out. We could have used it to go back to Villeneuve for good, but we didn't. We stayed." The princess didn't answer, but Belle could tell her words were sinking in.

"Don't let your anger at me stop you from saving your kingdom, Marianne," the Prince said. "I know what it's like to be so overpowered with grief and bitterness that they're a part of you. That's how I felt after my parents died."

The princess stared at the Prince. Belle squeezed her father's hand and hoped the Prince was getting through to his cousin.

"I was so lost back then," the Prince continued. "Lost in my own selfishness. I was convinced I was alone, and that no one was worse off than me. That's why I turned away your messenger before I even knew who had sent him. It wasn't until Belle came along that I realized I wasn't alone—that I'd *never* been alone."

He smiled at Cogsworth and Lumiere, who bowed in response.

"I wish I could go back in time and change things," the Prince told the princess. "Unfortunately, the Magic Atlas doesn't work like that. It can't help you fix the past. I only hoped it might be able to help me fix the present—and bring our family back together. But if you can't forgive me, I understand. Forget about me. Think about what *you* want."

"And what your mother would want," Belle added.

The princess walked over to the printing press. The sun had begun to rise, sending a silvery light through the window grate onto the machine's gleaming metal parts. "Even if it was possible"— she waved at the press—"the king would never …"

"Would never what?"

A gaunt man in a crimson jacket stood in the entryway, flanked by the two guards the Prince had transported out of the kingdom. They'd lost their helmets, and their hair was as disheveled as their uniforms. Their boots were covered in mud.

"Father!" Princess Marianne cried. "What are you doing down here?"

"I was awakened by these two fools," he said, indicating the guards, who cowered shamefully. "They had a wild tale of an enchanted book and being magically flown to the middle of the Sauvage Valley! They also told me about a crew of

interlopers who'd appeared in our kingdom out of nowhere. . . ." He looked around. "But I see the tale might not be so wild after all."

"It seems you did not transport them far enough, Your Highness," Lumiere whispered to the Prince.

"Maybe they're unusually fast walkers," Cogsworth suggested.

"We got a ride," the squeaky-voiced guard snapped.

"Ha!" barked the other, sneering at the Prince. "You didn't think we'd run into anyone in the middle of the night, did you? But it so happened there was a farmer out hunting for mushrooms, and—"

"Enough!" the king shouted. "Your story may be true, but you're still clods." He turned to the princess. "Marianne? Do you care to explain all this?"

Belle could tell from the silence in the room

that she wasn't the only one holding her breath. She, the Prince, Lumiere, Cogsworth, and her father stood so still they might have been statues.

"This is Queen Adele's son," Princess Marianne said finally, gesturing to the Prince.

The king glared at the Prince. "What is *he* doing here?"

"He came to apologize for not helping us, for turning away our messenger," the princess replied. "I locked him up, but he got out, along with the rest of them."

"How did I not know who was in my own dungeon?" The king cast an accusing look at his daughter.

Princess Marianne shook her head. "Because you've been locked away, too, by your own doing."

The king ignored her and turned to the Prince. "Your apology is worthless. It's come too late to—"

"He didn't know we'd sent the message," the princess said. "He didn't know about Mama."

"My mother had died, too," the Prince said. "And my father. And I . . . I hid behind my castle gates. I kept everyone out."

"Just like us," Princess Marianne said.

"Yes, well . . . we heard about Queen Adele," the king said softly. "I'm very sorry for your loss, but—"

"He wants to help now," the princess went on. "They *all* want to help. They think the printing press—"

"I stored these things away for a reason, Marianne!" the king snapped. "I never want to see any of it again."

"Then why did you keep it?" the princess asked.

The king hesitated. "Well . . . I couldn't just—"

"But you *could* have," interrupted his daughter. "You could have destroyed the books. You could have burned the paper and the wood from the printing press to warm the castle. You could have gotten rid of it all!"

"I intended to," the king said defensively.

"Someday . . . I just . . . I just forgot about it."

The princess shook her head. "I don't believe you. Throwing all this away would have been like throwing out my mother's dreams. You could have never done that. But leaving it here, Father—*Papa*—it's just as bad." Princess Marianne took the king's hand. "We can't bring Mama back to life," she said quietly. "But her dreams don't have to die."

The king was silent. He seemed torn. He glanced around the room at the press and the paper and the ink—the symbols of Queen Cecile's wish to bring books and learning to the kingdom's village.

"She'd be proud of what we're trying to do," the princess continued. "If we can make this machine work, we'll be able to print hundreds of books—not just for us, but for other cities and kingdoms, too."

King Robert finally met his daughter's gaze. "Do you really think it's possible?" he asked.

"I do, Papa. I really do."

The king let go of Princess Marianne's hand and walked to the press. He placed his hands on top of it and closed his eyes, fighting back emotion, as if touching it reawakened his memories of the queen and what the press had meant to her.

When he opened his eyes, he appeared changed. He was suddenly more regal, and hopeful. "Very well, then," said the king, addressing the group. "I command you all to get back to work."

Princess Marianne rushed to her father's side and embraced him. Belle and the Prince exchanged a smile. It seemed as if the king, like his kingdom, had been under a spell, and at last, the spell had been broken.

CHAPTER 19

The weather that day was foggy and rainy, as it usually was in the kingdom, which made it easy to collect enough water to test the new steam printing press. King Robert and Princess Marianne watched as the Magic Stone heated the water in the boiler.

The gears Maurice had added to the press

began to turn, moving the paper toward a thick woodblock, which pressed the paper onto the inked plate.

"Incredible!" King Robert exclaimed.

"It can press the ink onto paper faster than a person can do it," Maurice said. "But you still need people to cut the paper, set the type, and ink it."

"Luckily, you have a village filled with people who will be eager for the work," Belle said.

A few moments later, the block rose and the paper slid out. Princess Marianne joined Belle at the table, the paper facedown in front of them.

"Do you want to lift it up?" Belle asked the princess.

"Let's do it together."

Belle and Princess Marianne each took a corner. Together they drew back the paper, which was now dotted with black letters—letters arranged into words, sentences, paragraphs. . . .

"We made a book!" Princess Marianne cried.

"The start of one, anyway," Belle said. She held up the paper for the others to see. As she did, she caught a glimpse of the title. "It's *The Kingdom in the Clouds!*"

"Oh, yes . . . ," the princess said. "I remember my mother reading that to me when I was young. She probably thought it was one the children at the school would like, too."

"The author lives in your village!" Belle told her. "But it's not Pierre LeFaux." She told Princess Marianne and King Robert how Granny T had been swindled by LeFaux.

"Cecile would have been horrified!" King Robert said.

"We'll change the type on the title page and reprint it," Princess Marianne declared. "Then we'll print copies of the book for everyone in the village."

Later that day, King Robert and Princess Marianne finally ventured out from behind their gates. They traveled down the bumpy road to the village in their royal carriage, followed by Belle and her friends in "King Cogsworth's" carriage. This time, Belle got to sit inside.

There were a few clouds, but they were friendly and looked like cotton balls.

"The first thing we'll do once we have the funds is repair the roads," the king grumbled as he stepped out of his carriage into the village square. He helped Princess Marianne down. She squinted against the glare for a moment but then raised her shoulders and tilted her face toward the sky.

The villagers who'd seen the carriages approaching had gathered in the square, and stared in shock at their royal leaders standing before them. Belle glanced at Princess Marianne and King Robert and realized they were as uneasy as the villagers.

Suddenly, Elise burst out of the crowd with Petra on her shoulder.

"Belle!" she cried. "You broke the princess's spell!"

Princess Marianne blinked in surprise, then laughed. "She did." The princess smiled at Belle. "She really did."

Soon the princess and the king were strolling through the crowd, exchanging greetings with the villagers, answering questions, and sharing their plans to revitalize the kingdom and the village.

Monsieur LeFer offered to give the king a tour of his blacksmith shop. Maurice and the Prince went along to discuss the mass production of bookplates and type, a job the blacksmith and his two apprentices would soon be taking on.

Meanwhile, Cogsworth and Lumiere energetically offered their guidance to the villagers on how to fix up the square. Lumiere was especially intrigued by a space he thought would make a

perfect sidewalk café. Cogsworth shared his idea to install a clock in the roof of the bakery.

Belle led Princess Marianne over to Granny T. "This is the woman I told you about," she said as she introduced Granny T to the princess. "The author of *The Kingdom in the Clouds.*" Before they'd left the castle, they'd printed the title page and assembled the first several pages of the book. Princess Marianne now presented them to Granny T.

Granny T took the pages and gasped as she read the title page. "It's …" Her breath caught in her throat.

The princess nodded. "The name of the *true* author."

"Let me see!" Elise cried. Granny T handed her the pages. "It's you! It's your book!"

"It's only the first few pages," the princess said. "Once we have the press up and running in the village, we'll give you the whole book. We'll make

enough for any villager who wants one—and a copy for my father and me, of course, which I hope you'll sign."

"I'd be honored, Your Highness!"

Belle watched as Granny T stared down at the title page again, her eyes glistening with delight. Belle had never thought before what it would be like to see your own name on the cover of a book. She tried to imagine it and felt a chill go down her arms. How amazing that would be!

"Petra and I want one, too!" Elise declared, tilting her head toward her shoulder, where the little bird was watching the goings-on with bright, unblinking eyes.

The princess gently patted Petra's tiny head. "We'll give you the very first copy."

Before leaving the village, Belle told Elise and Granny T everything that had occurred at the castle. Elise was thrilled by every detail: Locked in a dungeon! Using a Magic Atlas to escape! And

of course, breaking the "spell" that had kept King Robert and Princess Marianne imprisoned by grief.

"You should write this as a story!" Elise told Granny T. "Then you'll have another book!"

"I would love to write another book, Elise," Granny T replied. "And I will. But what Belle told us isn't *my* story—it's hers."

She met Belle's eyes when she said this, and there was a notable spark in her expression— a challenge.

That night, King Robert and Princess Marianne hosted a dinner for Belle, Maurice, and the Prince. The princess insisted Cogsworth and Lumiere join them. The two servants couldn't help getting up from their seats repeatedly, however. Lumiere would rush off to the kitchen to check on the next

course, while Cogsworth took aside the guards-turned-waiters to remind them food is served from the right and drinks from the left.

As Belle ate, she thought about all that had happened since the moment Chip had found the music box. It had definitely been an adventure, one as exciting and memorable as any she'd read in a book. She remembered Granny T's challenge, and her mind wandered. . . .

"I'd like to place the first order for your press," the Prince told King Robert and Princess Marianne, interrupting Belle's thoughts. "A large order. For books for the library Belle is building in *our* village."

The king held up his glass. "I'd like something from you as well," he said to the Prince.

"Anything," the Prince answered. "I'll do whatever you ask if it will help make up for having failed you when you needed me."

King Robert paused a moment. "I'd like for us

to be a family again," he said. "Can we?"

"Yes! Yes! Of course!" The Prince burst out of his chair, arms wide—then caught himself. "I mean . . . it would, um, give me the greatest pleasure to—"

"Oh, get over here, young man," the king said. He stood and stretched out his own arms, one toward the Prince and one toward Princess Marianne.

Within seconds, the king held the two cousins in a tight embrace. Belle and Maurice clasped hands and watched the reunion with tears in their eyes.

"*Comme c'est formidable!*" Lumiere exclaimed, grabbing Cogsworth in a spontaneous hug.

Cogsworth hugged back before he realized what he was doing and broke free. He cleared his throat.

"Yes, yes. Wonderful indeed," he said, subtly wiping away a tear.

"Well, I think this calls for a celebration!" the king exclaimed as he let go of the Prince and princess. "What's for dessert?"

The others laughed. Belle smiled to herself. It was the perfect ending to a story. . . .

CHAPTER 20

"'Out of nowhere came a furious black cloud,'" Belle read in a hushed voice. "'A fierce wind swooped down and lifted the balloon from the castle roof. They found themselves rising up, up, up above the forest, into the sky. Michelle and her two friends clutched tight to the balloon's ropes. Together, they watched as the

castle grew smaller and smaller behind them....'"

Belle set the handwritten pages in her lap and looked nervously at her audience, seated on the large rug in the story time corner of the new library.

The village children stared up at Belle silently for a moment, and she felt a flicker of worry. If *they* didn't like it . . .

"Why did you stop?" asked a little girl.

The other children soon joined in: "What happens next?" "Keep going!" "Keep reading!"

Belle smiled, relieved and elated. They wanted to hear more! "That's all I've written so far," she told them. "But I'm glad you like it."

The children shouted out more questions, and their voices echoed against the mostly empty shelves lining the walls of the large room. Belle had received a shipment of adventure books from Paris and had brought down a selection of books from the castle library to lend, but these barely

took up a quarter of the space. She knew Princess Marianne and King Robert would be sending more books soon, however, and she looked forward to the day when every shelf was filled.

"Special delivery!" the Prince called from the entrance at the far end of the library. The children rushed for the door, and their parents quickly followed.

Once upon a time, Belle would have been the first—and maybe only—person in the village to greet the arrival of books so eagerly. Now she was the last one to leave the library, and she didn't mind at all.

When she stepped outside, she saw the Prince in front of several wagons stacked high with crates of books. As the children clamored around him, the Prince lifted down one of the crates and pulled off the top. "You can help take them in," he said, filling each child's arms with books. The adults pitched in to help.

"I'll show you which shelves to put them on," Belle told the villagers, but the Prince took her hand to stop her.

"I have another surprise for you," he said. A moment later, a figure emerged from behind one of the wagons.

"Granny T!" Belle hurried over to embrace her friend. "I can't believe you traveled all this way with the wagons!"

Granny T laughed. "Oh, no! I came a more exciting way—via a book!"

"As soon as I saw the wagons approaching, I took the Magic Atlas to Brumeuxville," the Prince told Belle. "Since we ordered copies of her books for all of your story time listeners, I thought you might like to have the author here to sign them."

"Thank you!" Belle hugged the Prince and then led Granny T into the library toward the story time corner, where the children were arguing over the arrangement of the new books. "This is the author

of my favorite book," she told the children.

"*The Kingdom in the Clouds!*" they yelled, clapping wildly.

"And she's brought a copy for each of you." The children swarmed Granny T, hugging her waist and shouting out their thanks.

Later, after Granny T had signed each child's book, Belle gave her a tour of the library. The Prince joined the children, sitting with them on the story time rug. He smiled as they showed him their favorite passages and illustrations. Ever since his reunion with his family, joy seemed to radiate from him. Belle now knew for sure that the Beast was gone.

"The Prince told me you've been working hard on your book," Granny T told Belle.

Belle blushed. "I'm trying."

"I'd love to read it when you're finished."

"I'm worried about that part," Belle said. "Finishing it, I mean. I thought I knew how to end

it, but now I'm not so sure. Fairy tales always wrap up so neatly. But real life . . . it just keeps going."

"Remember, a book is only one story," Granny T said. She tapped the spine of a book on the shelf next to her. "At the start, the heroine wants to achieve something. Once you've answered the question of whether she achieves it—that's the end. There might be new goals after that, but new goals mean new stories." She ran her fingers over the neighboring books.

Belle felt a scary sort of excitement as Granny T did this, dreaming of the day when a book she wrote might be sitting in this very library. She pictured it being borrowed by a girl just like her, who would sit alone on the edge of a village fountain somewhere, imagining herself in another world as she read Belle's words.

Belle lifted her gaze, taking in the entire library. She glanced from the now-filled stacks, to the Prince seated with her eager story time

listeners, to the children's parents and other adults, murmuring as they discussed the new books. Her mind wandered from there to King Robert and Princess Marianne, who were working together with their villagers to carry out the late Queen Cecile's dream.

Belle turned to Granny T. "I think I've answered the question."

Granny T took Belle's hand and they exchanged a smile, author to author. "Well, then—you've come to the end."